MARILIA G. BARBOSA

Copyright (c) 2020 Marília Galvão Barbosa

1st Edition
Tittle: The Duchess at Sea
Author: Marília Galvão Barbosa
Cover: Débora Silva
Editor: Faith Lane

All rights reserved.

All rights reserved. No parts of this book may be reproduced or transmitted in any form or by any means, electronic or mechanical, including photocopying, recording or by any information storage and retrieval system, without permission in writing from the publisher.

This is a work of fiction. Names, characters, places and incidents are either product of the author's imagination or are used factiously, and any resemblance to actual persons living or dead, businesses establishments or events is entirely coincidental.

Chapter One

My arm hurt as I was dragged down the deck. The man who had just found me went up the stairs to the quarterdeck and opened a door behind the wheel. Laughing, he threw me inside and I almost lost my balance.

"Look what I found, captain! I knew there was some food missing, and this girl is the bloody reason for it!"

The man sitting at the table was nothing like I had expected for a pirate captain. He had a short brown beard and straight bangs fell slightly over his eyebrows; he was incredibly neat despite the creased gray shirt. He slowly folded the paper he had been reading and put it inside the first drawer of the table as his honey eyes traced my body up and down. I hugged myself and stepped to the side, getting away from the man who brought me here.

The captain gestured for the man to leave and he complied, shutting the door. His shiny black boots were on the table, and he placed his intertwined fingers over his belly. I didn't dare speak a word.

"You got in at the last harbor two days ago, am I right?" I nodded in response. "Do you know we still have about five days to get to our next destination?" My answer was the same. "Well, we can't have you aboard and do nothing. You shall cook for us as payment."

I gulped and my voice was low. "I don't know how to cook."

He raised his eyebrows in fake surprise and his feet went to the floor so he could stand. Walking around the table, he approached me. Once he got too close, I stepped back until I hit the door.

"Well, I'm sure we can find some other use for a pretty girl like you on my ship."

A shiver ran down my spine, regretting my desperate choice at that harbor only two days ago, but what could I have done? They were about to find me, and the ship I had bought a room in had already set sail without me.

A stubborn tear slid down my cheek as I looked away.

"Oh, don't be like that." He grabbed one of my shaky hands. "I'm sure your soft, rich hands can survive washing the dishes for a few days." He laughed the moment my jaw dropped. "You are not to be harmed in my ship," he said and walked away. "You are very lucky I'm a gentleman, but what were you thinking, boarding a pirate ship? And alone, nonetheless."

Did he think I was stupid?

"I didn't know it was a pirate ship!" I hissed, and he turned a surprised look at me for speaking so assertively all of a sudden. "It looked like a nice, normal commercial vessel that was going to the city of Keanys," I remembered his words and then quickly added. "And I'm not rich."

As a pirate, I didn't doubt he was already thinking of ways to profit over me. Maybe that was his main reason to keep me unhurt, but I didn't want him to know my family was the richest in the country. I was already on a secret journey to ask for my grandfather's assistance and I didn't need to give him another trouble to handle. However, as he walked closer to me again with a smug smile on his lips, maybe I should promise him some money to guarantee I wouldn't get hurt until we reached our destination.

"Oh, you are. Maybe not much, but enough so you've always had someone cooking for you, isn't that right?" He carelessly grabbed the tip of my side braid, playing with my dark curly hair.

I stepped to the side, causing the strands slid away from his fingers. I had to hold the anger boiling within me. Who did he think he was to touch me like that?

"If it means anything, can I have your word that I won't be harmed?"

"You have my word." His tone was dead serious, and then he put a hand over his heart. "I am nothing but a gentleman."

I let out a laugh. "You're a pirate."

"I'm not only that, my dear."

"The name is Lenna," I lied. I wasn't willing to give him my real name.

"All right. Lenna. I'm Callum. You'll be sleeping in my cabin until we reach our destination."

"Thank you, but I'd prefer to sleep in the navigation room." I looked around. "I believe it's not taken during the night, right?"

"Not usually. But anyone can enter here at night, and although my crew is loyal and obedient, some are hard to control when they drink too much. I won't be there to stop them."

A shiver ran down my spine once again. I could stay alone in here with the possibility of anyone walking in—including that big guy who found me—or I could be in his room. At least I'd have only one person to worry about.

The latter didn't seem such a bad option. Although intrusive and arrogant, Callum was also polite.

"Fine, then...but don't touch me," I demanded.

"I'll keep my hands to myself." He laughed and raised his palms innocently. "And yes, of course, you're a rich folk, you demand just like one..." He opened the door. "Well, then, let me show you my ship." He extended his arm as a noble gentleman would. He just wouldn't waste a chance to mock me! I ignored the gesture and walked out by myself. He also stepped out of the navigation room and started leading me through a small tour around the ship.

It wasn't that different from other Galleon ships I've been to, there was the main deck with the forecastle in the front—where I was hidden with many barrels of foods and drinks for the two days, and where my satchel still waited for me. At the back, there was the sterncastle, with space for the officer's quarters and of course, the captain's quarters. Above it was the quarterdeck, the helm, and the navigation room.

We went downstairs to the gun and berth deck, where many cannons were displayed near the hatches and men slept on nets or improvised beds on the floor. At the front part was a room for the infirmary and gunpowder stock. At the back, there was the galley with two cooks working. There was another level downstairs for food stock and what I assumed was their treasures, since he told me I wasn't supposed to go further down. I didn't care, though.

"Now, it's time to introduce you to the crew," Callum said as he looked to a red-haired man approaching us.

"Nate told me about our unexpected guest." He turned to me. "I'm pleased to meet you, my lady." He bowed for a second, but I couldn't tell if he was sincere or if he was only teasing me.

"This is my best friend and second in command, Felix." Callum put a hand on his shoulder.

"I'm Lenna," I said.

"So it's true?" Another voice reached my ears right before I saw another guy coming towards us. He was wearing a red shirt, and he had an easy smile as he grabbed my hand to kiss it. I quickly pulled away. "It is like a dream to have a beautiful flower-like you aboard; a sight for sore eyes!"

"I'm obliged." I took a step back.

"By the way, I'm Enric, but you can call me Ric, or the man of your dreams if you will." He leaned closer; he had interesting copper skin and dark curly hair. He looked like the opposite of Felix.

Callum pushed Enric away from me, but the red hair was the one to speak. "I ask my humble apologies for my friend, he rarely knows how to act with the ladies."

"I think I'm supposed to wash some dishes, don't you agree, Captain?"

Felix choked a laugh, exchanging looks with Enric, I guess as if to say he had no chance with me this time. Callum suppressed his grin and nodded, taking me to the galley. He introduced me to the guys in the kitchen and after I was given some food, my dish-washing work began and I had to ignore the disgust for the rest of food.

When all the dishes were inside the cupboards that the cookers showed me, I walked around the ship. It was good to finally stretch my legs after spending two days hidden behind those barrels.

I expected everyone's eyes to follow me all the time, however, the feeling of being watched was still annoying. I crossed the gun deck and went up the stairs; the main deck was less full, which was a relief. There was nothing but the beautiful blue ocean and sky everywhere I looked. I still needed to get used to the movement of the ship, although it wasn't making me seasick. Stumbling around, I bumped into someone. The tall man glared at me; he had shoulder-length light brown hair and a beard.

"Lenna," he said.

I was about to ask how he knew my name since we hadn't been introduced, but I didn't need to. At this point, Callum must have told all the crew, and since I was the only girl aboard, it wasn't hard to know my name.

"Yes. And you are?"

"Alastair." Then, he just walked away, bumping my shoulder as he left showing he didn't care. How rude! He was more like the picture I had of a pirate. Anyway, I was glad he seemed to be the only one aboard who didn't care to look at me with hungry eyes. I'd have preferred all of them to do the same, staying away and ignoring me until we reached our destination.

Trying to get away from all the stares, I went to the only place I could be in closed quarters on this ship: the navigation room. Luckily, it was empty. I stayed there until it was time for dinner so I ate and started the dishwashing job once again.

When my task was finally over, the captain escorted me to his room at the sterncastle. His cabin was the last one; to go through it, we passed by a small corridor with four doors, they were the officer's rooms. I bet at least his best friend, Felix had one of those.

"Please, make yourself at home," Callum said. This was the last thing I wanted, but I remained silent as I entered.

The room was about the same size as the navigation

room; both had a little balcony at the back and a small door leading there as well. Big windows allowed me to look at the horizon, but he closed the curtains. There were also some cabinets on the wall under the windows. The bed was on the right side; it was big with drawers under it, and a shelf by its side, attached to the wall.

On the opposite side, a huge drawer stood with a jar of water and bathing things lying around; at least he had some hygiene habits, or so it seemed. Near the window, there was a long sofa. A small table stood in the middle of the room with a chair. Callum opened a drawer under his bed and grabbed some blankets, giving them to me.

"Enjoy your stay." He gestured at the sofa.

I was happy it was way more comfortable than the floor behind the barrels in the forecastle. I left my satchel under the sofa with the few clothes I had and took off my boots before I lied on the sofa. Using a folded blanket as a pillow and the other to cover me. Callum blew off the fire in the lamp on the table; the dim moonlight around the curtains barely allowed me to view him as he changed his clothes before he lay down on his bed.

"Aren't you going to change, my lady?"

"I am fine as it is."

"Alright then." He shrugged. "One more thing, if you get scared at night, all you have to do is cross the room." He mocked me.

I frowned and turned to face the opposite side. My tone came out more sarcastic than I had intended.

"I'm obliged with your offer, though it's completely unnecessary."

He laughed but didn't say anything else. And then the room fell dead silent, apart from the wood clicking from time to time and the seawater against the ship.

Chapter Two

I couldn't sleep, so I threw the blankets to the side and stood up from the couch, I silently exited the captain's quarters, leaving Callum asleep in his bed. I strolled down the main deck and reached the forecastle. I went up and supported my arms on the taffrail. The cool gentle breeze brushed against my hair, making some curly strands leave the braid and fly free in the wind. The moonlight made my skin look bluish and looking at my strange-hands; I felt like I was someone different. For a moment, I was pretending to be as free as the other people in the ship, but I was only fooling myself. They could come and go as they pleased, not bound to stupid contracts like I was.

The dark sea met the navy blue sky in the distance, blending in a way it was almost impossible to tell which one was which. If it weren't for the stars above and the moon gleam on the water.

"Why must you give me so much trouble?"

Distracted with the darkness around, I only noticed someone was near me when he leaned over the taffrail by my side. I jumped in surprise.

"And why do you wish to give me a heart attack? Do

you want to kill me?"
"If I wanted it, I wouldn't wake up in the middle of the night and get up from my bed, Lenna." Callum pinched the bridge of his nose.
"I'm fine here, you know. You don't have to stick around every second while I'm on board. The crew is sleeping, anyway."
"The only way I can guarantee to keep my word is if I've got an eye on you all the time."
"Didn't you say your crew was obedient?"
"Didn't I tell you I can't control their every movement?"
"Or maybe you're just around because I'm the closest thing you have to entertainment on this ship?"
"I can't deny there's a bit of truth in there." He shrugged. "After all, there is no other woman aboard and something different is always interesting."
I rolled my eyes. I didn't expect anything different, but then again, he wasn't that boring himself. Callum was smart—smarter than I expected a pirate to be. He not only knew how to read, but he knew the language pretty well since he barely made mistakes for as long as we have spoken. In fact, come to think of it, some members of the crew had the same characteristics, or so I've heard them speaking at the galley.
"Will you stop looking at me like that?"
"Like what?" I hadn't even realized I was analyzing him until he spoke. Although I noticed the scar on his chin and how wide his shoulders were.
"This intense look you have in those greenish-blue eyes that look like the shallow waters of Desllan beaches."
I've never been to Desllan, but I've heard it was a beautiful place.

"Thanks."

"I didn't mean it as a compliment, it's...disconcerting."

My jaw dropped, and I turned away, frowning my eyebrows.

"Sorry, I didn't mean to upset you. I've been out of practice talking to women." I kept silent and he leaned close enough so I could feel his warm breathing over my shoulder. "And I'm tired, thus not thinking straight." His hand tried to touch mine, but I quickly crossed my arms to avoid it.

"No one is stopping you."

"You will make me mad halfway through our journey, is it what you want?" I remained silent. "Why are you here in the middle of the night, anyway? Aren't you sleepy?"

"I'm tired, yes, but I don't want to sleep—at a time like this when almost everyone is unconscious—is when I feel the freest." And it's also when I can walk around without being stared at all the time.

"Is it that you're looking for in Keanys?"

"Yes, and no...but you wouldn't understand. You've got everything you want, you can go wherever you feel like. All you need is the wind on your sails and the sea to conquer."

"Not exactly..."

"What do you mean?"

"I've always known that being a pirate was temporary. After Keanys, I'll lead this ship to one more trip and then I'll retire."

"Aren't you too young for that?"

"Retire of pirating. Not other things. I've received a letter from my mother and there are some things I need to do."

"Oh, so you have a family."

"Of course, don't you?"

"Well, yes, but I never thought people like you would have..."

He laughed, supporting his head on his fist. "You are quite judgy, you know that?"

"You can't tell me you didn't have misconceptions about being a pirate before you became one. Or about anything else." I shrugged. "And why have you chosen it in the first place?"

"My brother and I had a huge fight about ten years ago. That was when I decided to leave my home. Some very good friends followed me, and we ended up agreeing to have this lifestyle for the fun of it."

"Your ideas about recreational activities are quite amusing."

"I'm flattered." He dramatically put a hand on his chest. "So what exactly are you trying to get from this trip? Are you planning to get back home?"

"Yes, but as the owner of my own choices."

"How so?"

I wondered for a moment if I should tell him or not. I didn't know how dangerous it'd be for him to know everything; therefore, I needed to be cautious about what I'd say.

"My uncle wants to take everything that belongs to me by making me marry and when I do that, this union will take away the rights to what my family owns. My uncle is the next in line, so he'll inherit everything as soon as I marry. And I don't even know the guy!"

I slammed my fists onto the taffrail, the same anger from the moment my uncle told me the news was boiling inside me.

"You're rich." He pointed out as if that was the only part he paid attention to.

"Please, you already knew that." He just didn't know how rich or who I really was.

"How rich?"

It was almost like he'd read my mind. "It doesn't concern you."

"Why are you going then? Asking for a lover's help?"

"What? No. There's no one like that. I just hope that a family member might help me out in getting away from this stupid marriage."

My grandfather was my only hope at this point, and uncle Oliver wouldn't let me go there, that was why I had to dress as a peasant and leave the castle and the city as soon as I could.

Eventually, tiredness got the best of me and I agreed to go to sleep.

As I exited the captain's quarters the next morning, I nearly bumped into someone exiting an officer's room. It was that tall guy with long hair and beard; again, he just glared at me and left. I still had about an hour before I had to go to the galley, so once again, I went to the navigation room. It wasn't empty this time, though. The blond man lifted his head from the maps and smiled, adjusting his glasses.

"Lenna." He stood up, revealing the beautiful navy blue vest with golden buttons over his white shirt. "I haven't had the pleasure to meet you, yet." He extended a hand to me.

Instead of moving forward to accept his handshake, I

only did a quick curtsy in greeting. He saw my discomfort and sat down again.

"My name is Hayden. Please take a seat if you will. I'm nearly done; therefore, I'll soon be on my way."

I chose a chair on the opposite side of the table.

"What are you doing here, Hayden?"

"I'm the navigator and manager of this ship. I not only guide us through the water but also put everyone in their places."

"Seems like you do all the important work, then." I glanced at the map; he was probably calculating the time we'd take to arrive at Keanys.

"Basically, but half of my job is to tell people what to do and guarantee everything is in order. I like it: makes the journeys not so boring."

"I see…and are you also the one to calculate the crew's profits?" I took my chance to get to know them a little further.

He smiled. "No, that would be Felix and Callum. Ric takes care of the commodities we transport and Al takes care of our security."

"Al?"

"Pardon me, I mean Alastair."

He was the big guy from earlier.

"Oh, yes, I've met him. But so you transport commodities as well. That's why I mistook you with a regular mercantile ship. I don't understand, though. If you're pirates, you aren't supposed to be welcomed so easily at harbors and you shouldn't want to risk being caught."

"We are not pirates to all countries. We help the ones we want to and thus we have no problem in those regards as we dock on such places, Alleara being one of them."

They probably didn't start off as pirates; they were

the crew of a common trading vessel at first. I've heard pirates were often rebelling crews.

"Speaking of which, most of you seem to come from Alleara. Or so the similar accents of the five or you suggest."

"Indeed, we are; hence the fact we like the country." Hayden stood up, collecting his maps. He put everything away in a drawer at the wall. "See you later, Lenna." He waved as he exited and closed the door.

I leaned on the chair, enjoying my brief hour of loneliness. I stood up to observe the wooden ship miniature on the shelf as I let my thoughts wander around.

Despite the fact I barely knew them, the crew seemed to be quite nice, and they hadn't done anything or said anything inappropriate to me. They only stared at me. The officers with whom I spoke to also seemed interesting. Well, most of them. Alastair was silent, keeping his distance, which was appreciated. Enric was the total opposite, he was talkative and charming, although didn't nag, coming after me as much as I thought he would when we were introduced.

Then there was Felix, the red-head and Hayden. They seemed to be the biggest gentlemen of the group and were good to talk to. I still didn't really know what to think of the captain. He was nice and mostly polite, however, I still didn't know the reason behind his intentions.

Once my free time was out, I had to come down to the gun deck again to eat and do my job.

CHAPTER THREE

The sunlight was so bright as I exited the gun deck that it blinded me for a second. But, my hands shaded me with enough protection until I adjusted to the brightness of the afternoon in the middle of the ocean. The heat from the sun was comfortable on my hands; they were freezing after spending so much time washing the dishes.

Sitting on the ground, leaning on the taffrail behind him, Felix was writing in a journal. He was enjoying the sail's shade; I imagined it was hard for him to stand under the sun for so long with such a pale skin full of freckles. He wasn't too concentrated, looking around constantly. I walked over to him and sat by his side, yet keeping my distance.

"Good afternoon." I started. "Are you documenting today's events?"

He chuckled. "No. Hayden or Callum, maybe, but I don't really do that. There is no reason to document anything, especially on such an ordinary day. Why do you ask?"

"You were looking around and the five of you all have specific duties on the ship, right?"

"I see you've been talking to Hayden, haven't you?"

"Yes, I have." He must know him very well to assume it with such conviction. "You have known each other for a long time, don't you?"

"Indeed, we do. I was born in Ellinis, but my parents moved to the capital when I was about ten. That's when the five of us met."

If I remembered the maps well, Ellinis was the land in the furthest north part of our country; dad said their plain fields were beautiful, I wish Dad had taken me there.

"It was a long way south." I pointed out.

"It was worth it." He shrugged.

I glanced at the notebook in his hands. "So what are you doing? I mean, if you don't mind me asking."

"Not at all." He handed me the book with charcoal drawings on the white pages. "I'm just seizing the day by exerting myself to carry out my hobbies."

The picture on the page was incomplete, but beautiful nevertheless. It portrayed some crew members wiping the floor on the other side of the deck.

"You're an artist!" I looked at him. "May I see the rest of it?"

"Please, be my guest."

I flipped through the pages, taking the time to look at each page. Most of them were various crew members in the ship and his friends. It made sense. Since they spent so much time at sea, there wasn't much to copy in the middle of nowhere. There were some drawings of ships as well, and some of the diverse people in varied cities.

"Those are so beautiful!"

"I'm obliged." He smiled. "What I enjoy the most is to portray people, it's a challenge to copy their souls on the page, but at the same time, I also like just picturing daily situations."

"Or different places. You've probably seen so many of them!"

"Yes, we have had the opportunity to see many cities and countries."

My smile didn't reach the eyes.

"I wish I could have this privilege." The words came out on their own before I could have time to stop them.

"Perhaps in the future?" he suggested, optimism covering his words in a gentle way.

"I hope." I handed him his journal and changed the subject. "And do you think you could draw me?"

"Of course. Lovely ladies are a great delight to portray."

He opened a blank page and started his work. I stayed there until it was time for dinner.

My back hurt from leaning over the cupboard the entire evening, doing the dishes in the washbasin. I almost regretted not sleeping more, but I kinda enjoyed last night and that made me happy. Tonight, however, it was like they couldn't stop eating. The clean dishes were disappearing from the cupboard faster than I could wash them again. I only had time for a short break in the afternoon, but now the noisy pirates wouldn't stop drinking, eating, and laughing. I was almost sure they were doing it on purpose to mock me, after all. I was there for so long I didn't even have time to have dinner.

Someone left more dirty plates and cutlery by my side, and I was under the impression he had put dirty dishes for me earlier. I sighed, unwilling to let them irritate me. I was also scared to say something and end up making it worse. I only had a few more days to endure, anyway.

One of the pirates came closer. He was the man who found me, the biggest one of the group. He was as wide as a wardrobe. From behind me, he added his dish on the pile and rested his big hand on the counter, leaning closer. With no way out, I pressed myself against the counter so I would at least not touch his body, however, it didn't work. He just took a step closer. He put the other hand on the opposite side of the counter, trapping me in place.

"Hey, pretty..." He said in a slurred way and the stink of rum made me wonder just how many bottles he had drank.

"Get away from me."

I leaned away as far as I could and even tried to push him away with an elbow, but he was like a wall and didn't move an inch. One of his hands touches the curve between my neck and shoulder, descending to the collarbone of my peasant white shirt. He slowly pushed it down.

"Stop it!" I slapped his hand. He laughed, and the foul smell coming from his mouth almost made me throw up.

I grabbed a knife from inside the washbasin and slid it against his hand when he kept messing with my shirt. The cut was small and probably didn't even bother him since he just laughed looking at the thin trace of blood.

"Feisty!" He smiled at me and clasped my wrist, twisting it until I was forced to let go of the knife in my hand.

He pulled me closer, way faster than I had expected a drunk guy could, pressing me against his body. I tried to pull him away, but all my strength wasn't enough to move him a millimeter. I was fairly sure I had screamed when he leaned in to kiss my shoulder, but I was too desperate to register what I was doing besides pushing him away and trying to free my right wrist from his iron grip.

Next thing I knew, he was being pulled away from me by many hands and someone entered in front of me.

"What's wrong with you?" Callum pushed the man on the chest, making him step back.

I panted, feeling dizzy. They took him away, and Callum turned to face me.

"Come. Enough cleaning for you tonight." He gently held my shaky hands and guided me up to the main deck. I didn't know how I managed to walk with legs so wobbly, but somehow we arrived at his cabin. "I'm sorry for Nate's behavior, he has this tendency to think he can do anything, especially if he had way too many drinks."

Callum checked the water jar on the dresser.

"You may wash yourself if you want to." He put something on my hand, which was shaking less. "I'll be back in an hour, but you may lock the door meanwhile."

He left the room so fast it took me a while to understand he had given me the key to the door. I immediately locked it and washed myself to get rid of any trace of Nate's touch or smell on me. I put on the simple nightgown from my satchel and only opened the door to Callum. I had thought about seizing the room all to myself; but after what had just happened, I actually wanted the captain's constant presence around me. I was sure he wouldn't do anything like that, nor let anyone get close like that again.

Callum closed the door, and I lied down on my improvised bed on the other side of the room. As he took off his boots and lied on his bed, he apologized once more.

"Nate will apologize as well and he will be punished." He assured me. "Once he's sober."

"Was that why you were lurking me all the time? You

knew he'd try to do something when he had a chance?"

"I knew it was possible for most of them to try their chances on you, but indeed, Nate was the first that came to mind in a list of possible suspects. He's strong, impulsive and he's used to having all the women he can pay for pleasureful services in front of him."

"But I don't get it. I didn't get close to him, I didn't even talk to him to make him pay attention to me."

"He'd pay attention to any pair of boobs in front of him..." He cleared his throat. "I mean, to any feminine curves around."

"He's disgusting. And he had no right to do what he did!"

"I know and I agree, but what do you want me to do? It's not like I can control his every move, and it also wouldn't be right to do so if I could. All I can do is set the rules and hope everyone will choose to follow them." He sighed heavily. "And of course, he might give excuses like growing up in a bad environment, being drunk, or not having a good moral sense. Which all do apply to Nate, but in the end, choosing to do the right thing is on him."

"Yes, but he won't do it. As you said, he thinks he can do anything he wants. I bet it's because he's stronger and gets things done his way already. But being strong doesn't give men the right to get their way on women, and it doesn't give him the right to hit me either."

The words just flowed out my mouth, the fury bottled up inside for many years burst in an instant. Callum raised his body, supporting his weight on an elbow so he could look at me.

"Are we still talking about Nate? Because he didn't hit you."

"I was talking in general."

"Seemed pretty specific to me." Ignoring him, I turned to face the wall. "Lenna… has your uncle hit you?"
I decided to change the focus of the topic.
"You're not like that at all…" I turned just enough to see him. "I wonder why."
He fell for it as he lay back down, facing the ceiling.
"I wouldn't like any harm to come to my mother, nor would I like to any sisters or daughters, if I had any. So I don't think it'd be fair to do it to others. Besides, my dad used to say that a man who has to force his way into a woman wasn't doing the job right…not that I understood exactly what he meant at the time, I was a child when he passed away. His words stuck to me, though; and with time the understanding did too."
"I'm sorry about him. He seemed like a great man."
"He was the greatest of the land." By the nostalgic sound of his voice, I imagined he had a sad smile on his lips.
"And you seem to be following his steps pretty well." I adjusted myself to be more comfortable. "Good night, Callum."
Soon I let myself be dragged to dreamland, too tired to fight my heavy eyelids this time.

CHAPTER FOUR

I could hardly believe the sight in front of me as I exited the captain's quarters the next day. Nate was standing in the middle of the deck; Callum by his side, crossing his arms and on the other, Alastair was glaring at the man between them.

"I'm sorry if I scared or hurt you last night, Milady. The event will not be repeated."

My eyes widened at it.

"Dismissed," Callum commanded in the end. Nate nodded and walked away. The captain then turned to face me. "As I said, you shall not be harmed in my ship."

"Thank you." I heard myself speak, but I was still so astounded that my brain wasn't working properly.

I was aware of the fact that Callum was respected and obeyed, but I didn't expect him to make one of the largest men on the ship apologize to me like that. However, the most surprising thing was Callum's determination in making me feel good in our journey. I was only a clandestine. I wasn't paying them; he knew I was somewhat rich. He was not getting anything out of this, so he definitely didn't need to go through such lengths to please me.

Callum continued, grasping me away from my thoughts.

"If anyone does or says anything inappropriate to you from now on, you may immediately report it to Al and he will sort it out."

I'd rather tell Callum himself, or even Felix or Hayden, but I knew it was because Alastair was in charge of the ship's safety.

"Alright," I answered.

"Now, let's have breakfast. I'm hungry."

I followed him close behind, unwilling to stand alone in the ship anymore, despite his efforts in making me feel safe.

After having a small loaf of bread with some butter, I started my task. Breakfast was always slow. The crew would take a while to wake up and eat, but I also had fewer dishes because some men would sometimes only grab fruits or eat bread with no plates. When finished, I went to the navigation room until it was time for lunch again.

I was starting to get bored at this routine but kept reminding myself it'd be for a short amount of time.

As I concentrated on washing, Callum surprised me by leaning on the cabinet by my side as he faced the galley.

"Would you join Felix and me for a card game after dinner?"

"I have my job to do."

"Not anymore. Nate will wash it at night and he'll have extra watching shift as well of other tasks he hates doing. At least for three days as his punishment, then we'll get other people to do it as usual. That'll teach these men to respect a lady; they shouldn't have been pranking you last night."

So I was right, they were pranking me! I wanted to

break these plates in each of their heads for this!

Callum crossed his arms and continued. "Besides, after spending the entire day drinking their rum, they're more likely to do something stupid like that again at night. So it's best for you to be away from here. You may stay in my room if you wish, but you could enjoy yourself and have a more entertaining evening if you come with us."

I smiled.

"I'm obliged and I gladly accept your invitation."

"Good."

Someone came to put more dirty dishes on the pile and left. I glanced at Callum, still standing there, looking at the entire gun deck behind my back.

I put my sleeves up again; they kept sliding down and getting wet in the water inside the washbasin.

"Callum, may I ask you a question?" My voice was softer than I expected.

"Isn't that already a question?" He smiled.

I rolled my eyes; ignoring his joke, I proceeded.

"Why are you so determined to keep me safe and well? I mean, you're here right now to guarantee it, aren't I right?"

He sighed. "I told you, many members of the crew are drunk all the time and—"

"Yes, I know." I cut him off. "You've told me this before. What I mean is, the reason why you want to keep me safe."

He was taken aback. "Isn't it obvious? This is my ship and I want everyone here to be safe."

"Oh..." I trailed off without even thinking, my attention back to washing.

"What? Why the disappointment?" He stepped

closer.

"I'm not disappointed!"

"Of course you are, it's in your face! What's the problem? Aren't you happy here? Don't you feel safe?"

"Yes."

"So what's wrong?"

"I guess I expected more from you, that's all."

"What do you mean?" His voice was indignant.

"Well, you only want to keep me safe because I'm on *your* ship. So, if you saw one of them doing something wrong to me on land, that'd be fine? Or if it was something against a child or an elderly?"

"What...no!"

"So would you stop them if that was the case?"

"In fact, I've done that before." Pride washed over his words as he pointed at his chest.

"Good, but why? Was it just a sense of duty?"

"Maybe. What's wrong with it?"

I put more clean dishes to the side and picked up the last dirty ones. I moved without even thinking, my hands were already used to the task; I glared at the captain. Knowing his positive traits were nothing more than some sort of prideful ownership was rather disappointing.

"The problem is that you should do it because it's the right thing, not because of duty or pride. If you do something good only to tell others you've done something good, does that make you an honorable man? No."

"Why not? I am doing everything I can!"

"For the wrong reasons."

I knew I should just stop talking; I was pretty lucky here, however, learning that all of that was nothing a little deeper than the eyes was so frustrating! He could have fooled me into thinking he was a good man.

"Does that make any difference?"

"Of course! An honorable person strives to do the right thing and doesn't need to tell people about their good deeds." I sighed. For a moment, I thought he was like that, but no, he just wanted to brag about how good he was.

He opened and closed his mouth a few times, trying to say something, but couldn't. Then he looked away. He looked so lost I almost felt sorry for him. Maybe uncle Oliver was right; I really had this tendency of talking too much.

"I'm sorry, I exceeded myself a little..."

"No." He shook his head and his voice sounded hoarse. "You're right. I've just forgotten it." He shrugged. "I guess sometimes we're so focused on our daily lives it's easy to forget what really matters or what *should* matter. You know, my dad used to say a person only shows their true self when people aren't looking. But I'm usually so concerned with my appearance I forget to be who I truly want to be."

As I finished washing everything, I grabbed a cloth to dry the plates and put them in the cabinet above my head. I had to stretch myself to put the plates in there.

I could feel his eyes on me and my sleeves slid from gravity, now going the opposite way of what I wanted them to be when I was washing. The right side descended until it showed my elbow, so I quickly put my arms down. I didn't have time to adjust them, though; Callum's sharp eyes had spotted what I didn't want him to see. He grabbed my arm with a hand while the other held the sleeve up so he could examine the purplish spot there. It had almost vanished by now, turning an ugly greenish yellow shade.

"Was that Nate?"

A shiver ran down my spine, and I pushed his hands

away from me. Luckily, he didn't try to stop me, bringing his hands to himself.

"No. I had this before I came aboard the ship. I had fallen in my house a day before I decided to go on this journey."

"It doesn't seem like a falling wound."

"I don't care what you think. I speak the truth and you have nothing to do with it."

I resumed my task and was relieved when he backed away, noticing how tense I was. Of course, I hadn't said the truth, but I didn't want any nosy pirate acting as if he cared or wanted to help. I didn't need anyone's help, and I needed to prove it if I hoped to ever be able to command my lands. There was nothing he could do anyway, so I wanted to keep my problems to myself. He should respect that.

Callum remained silent as I finished putting away the dishes and then escorted me to the navigation room, where Hayden was checking his maps.

CHAPTER FIVE

The afternoon ended soon and as soon as we finished having dinner, the three of us went back to the navigation room. I didn't want to admit it, but my heart was booming in joy. Not only because I wouldn't be stuck at the galley for hours, but also because the promise of an evening with games was amusing. I hadn't played any games for at least seven years, after all.

"So what shall we play? What do you usually do on these occasions?"

Callum smiled, and with only a glance, he told Felix to get the games. The captain positioned a chair at the head of the table so I could sit there. He sat by my side after he got three metal glasses from a shelf and a bottle of wine from a chest in the corner of the room.

Felix walked to one of the shelves and got a small wooden box from there, opening it as he sat by my left side. He set a pack of cards in the middle of the table, his pale fingers mixing them up.

"It's been a while since I've played card games, so you'll have to remind me of the rules."

"Don't worry, I have something easy in mind..." Felix had a sly smile on his lips.

"Not again." Callum laughed as he rested his chin on his hand.

"Come on, it'll be fun with a new person around."

"I'm sorry, what is it?" I was looking at Felix for the answer, but it actually came from the other side.

"It's a guessing game."

"Called Bullsh—" Felix started, but was quickly cut off.

"Please, Felix, we have a lady among us tonight."

"I mean Cheat." He corrected himself. "It's simple, the goal is to run out of cards and all you have to do is get some cards and discard them in the middle saying which are they. If we suspect you, we call the name's game."

"And let me guess, if the guesser is wrong or if the liar is caught, they get the cards in the middle, right?"

Felix cheered and pointed at me.

"That's it, girl!" So he started the game, discarding some cards. I didn't call it a bluff, and neither did Callum, who was the next player.

"I have here three A's." He looked at me as he placed the cards in the middle. His eyes were suspicious somehow, squinting slightly as if he was daring me.

"Bullshit," I called out before I could stop myself, and his jaw dropped as he heard the word. I shrugged. "What? I know the word. Thanks for being polite, though."

"So we go with that name." Felix giggled after a moment of surprise.

Callum sighed and grabbed all the cards in the middle. Then it was my turn, and we continued the game. Felix called out a bluff from me, but he was in the wrong and took the cards and both Callum and I laughed.

As we played, Felix turned out to be an expert at it. He not only knew at least 90% of the times Callum was

lying, but he also frequently knew when I was bluffing. It was no surprise he won the game in the end.
"So why didn't you want to play it at first?" I asked the captain.
"It's not that it's boring, it's just that it's not that challenging." Callum raised his hands, palms facing up.
"We know each other far too much," Felix explained. "So we know when the other is lying pretty easily, however, having a new player to shake things up makes for a rather amusing game."
"Which I agree," Callum said.
I hid my smile behind the card in my hand. Indeed, I haven't had that much fun in a while. Felix started gathering the cards.
"How did you meet? Was it all of you at the same time?"
"No, it wasn't, I was the first, though. Our mothers wanted us to be friends."
"As any sane children, we were against it, of course," Callum said. "It all changed when we began sharing the same hatred for an annoying teacher."
"He says a teacher, but he was more like a coach." There was something off in Callum's eyes; it was almost the same as when he'd called the three A's bluff. "He wanted to teach us how to fight, but he was so bossy. I believe he delighted himself in hurting other people."
"So we both pranked the man, putting grass in his underpants. Well, I did it while Felix was distracting him." Callum's shoulders shook as he laughed. "And of course, he punished us later, but it was fun."
"You know what they say if two people hate each other, nothing better than giving them a common enemy so they can hate it together."

31

"Well, it worked!"

"Indeed. And later came Enric, followed by Alastair and Hayden who were the last one to join."

"We were more open to receiving them, though. After all, if we had much fun with only two, imagine what a bunch of kids would do…" Felix shrugged playfully.

"Give me one example, then. What did the five of you do that was so fun?"

"There was that time in the kitchen," Felix said and Callum's eyes screamed he knew exactly what he meant, but there was a hint of fear in them as soon as he heard my next question.

"Kitchen? Like a regular kitchen from one of your old homes?"

"No, it was a big kitchen."

"From a very large tavern." Felix completed way too quickly. "In our village."

"Yes. They made a wonderful apple pie, and we wanted that. So, once they made some of them for an event, we spent hours plotting how to get there, because there were always people around and our parents had forbidden us to go there."

"So we sneaked out of our rooms at night, avoiding people passing by, and we headed there. Hayden and Al stayed at the door to guard us while the rest of us searched for two pies. Then we all hid to eat."

"Our parents were so mad at us when they found out…"

"It was totally worth it, though."

"Don't you have stories like these, Lenna?"

"Unfortunately, not. I'm afraid I was too well behaved when I was a child. However, I did have fun with my friends."

"They can't be that fun if you didn't play games or do pranks with them for so long. I mean, what else is there to do?"

I forced my smile this time.

"Unfortunately, I haven't seen them for a while and when I rarely do, we usually just talk. We don't really have time for games anymore."

I miss my friends. But they were getting married now, some were having children, even. I wish I could see them, visit them, or at least have them come to visit. However, Oliver doesn't let them. It's easier to control prey when it's lonely.

"Oh, I'm sorry about it, then..." Felix's voice was sincere, but I still didn't like it when he reached to my hand. I knew it was just a comforting gesture, but I hate having my personal space invaded like that by people I barely know. Even if he was a true gentleman, I slowly retrieved my hands closer to myself.

"It's alright. I will make time for them soon and then we can play it." I gestured at the cards.

Felix agreed while Callum stared at me, his face was serious and he was so attentive it was like he wanted to read my thoughts. I stood up.

"I'm tired now, so I'm going to the cabin if you don't mind."

"Be my guest." Callum gestured to the door and so I left.

Chapter Six

In the morning, I didn't find Callum in his room or at the galley, so it wasn't really a surprise to see him in the navigation room with Hayden after breakfast. Both had frowns and their voices were tougher than usual. But I only noticed it after I had opened the door, making them cut off in mid-sentence.

"I'm sorry, I didn't mean to interrupt…"

"It's alright." Callum gestured me to come in. "We're just talking."

Although I didn't know if I should enter or not, my legs were persuaded to enter, complying with his unspoken welcome. I decided to keep my distance. So instead of sitting at the table with them, I walked around, admiring the ship miniatures as Hayden continued to talk.

"The problem with that is Enric spotted a ship last night. We were lucky he changed the route so fast, otherwise, we could have been seen."

"It'd only be a problem if it was a foreign navy ship." Callum rubbed his short beard as he thought out loud.

"Which is likely," I said before I could stop myself.

Callum squinted his eyes. "Why do you say that?"

"Sorry, I shouldn't meddle in it…" I stepped back.

"That's not a problem, Lenna, but why do you say that?"

I gulped, but I came forward.

"I know there are some navy ships from Estanya around here." I pointed at the map around Keanys and up. "I've heard that a wealthy duke was coming here for a business meeting with a noble in the region. He's very careful and worried, so he asked his king to have the navy patrol the area for...pirates."

"How do you know that?" Callum asked.

I bit my lower lip. I've heard Oliver talking about it with the man who brought the news two days before I left. The man was talking about possible delays of shipments from my lands to this region because of that. However, I couldn't say it.

"I've heard it at the docks before I entered the ship. Haven't you heard it?"

"No, we haven't. Thank you, though." His honey eyes blinked at me. "We shall be more careful from now on. Estanya is a complicated country in which we have robbed many times before, their navy hates us." He turned to the blond man. "Find possible safe routes so we have options if we need to change and tell the guys about it later."

"Aye, captain," Hayden answered, then he turned to me and surprised me by asking what I thought of the routes he was taking as he showed them on the map.

"I know that the duke is traveling with two navy ships and that it's possible that there's going to have intense navy traffic around the cities he's visiting." I pointed to the cities I remember being discussed, Keanys was between the last two.

Hayden thanked me and put his attention on the map, planning the safest route possible with the new information.

I was washing the dishes after lunch when Alastair's deep voice echoed around the gun deck.

"Come on, lazy assholes! Get your bloody bodies to work. You need to practice more. I'm tired of seeing you all lying around uselessly all day!"

Faster than I'd have imagined, everyone in the deck stood up, grabbing their swords to practice fighting in pairs. Curious, I kept distracting myself, looking over my shoulder at the men fighting behind me. I was astounded to see how they moved so swiftly and precisely. It was almost like a dance, a very deadly dance with pointy blades smashing against each other.

Alastair walked around the group of men, telling them how to improve their fighting. The pairs would change constantly and eventually, Alastair turned to one of his friends, challenging him. Enric took off his dark red jacket and drew his sword. Soon they began a fight. They were so quick I stopped washing to observe them better; yet, it was all so fast I could hardly follow their movements. Alastair won all the attempts, and now I knew why he was the one to take care of the safety of their ship.

Callum stood up from the bench in the galley, leaving his coat behind and lifting his sleeves, challenging the big guy. They fought as well, and although Callum lasted longer than Enric in a more amazing fighting practice, he ended up losing. Either way, the men paying attention to it cheered; I didn't know if it was because he lasted long or if they just wanted to give some moral support to their leader.

Enric came to the galley and drank a cup of water from the barrel in the corner, which reminded me I still had my task to fulfill, so I turned around to finish it.

"So, enjoyed the show?" Enric's voice came behind me, his breath brushing against my hair.

"Yes, it was fun." I stepped to the side, getting away from him. He didn't take the hint, though.

"Good. Did you like my performance?"

I shrugged. "I don't believe I'm qualified to analyze sword fighting performances."

He smiled, reaching out to touch my arm.

"Oh, but I'm sure you—"

"Give her some space, she's working." Callum pushed Enric away from me, then grabbed a cup to fill it with water to drink.

I finished the washing part and began putting everything away in the cabinets.

"You've all been friends for a long time, right?"

"Indeed," Callum answered.

"I believe you also have trained together, right?"

"For the most part, yes. Why?"

"I was just wondering. Why is Alastair so much better than you all?" I was curious and distracted looking at the people still practicing and the big man helping them that it took me a while to notice I was rather impolite.

"Hey, this was the time I lasted the most!" His voice bore an indignant tone underneath it, but his smile betrayed him. "I am quite good as well."

"I'm sorry, I didn't mean to upset you." Every dish was now in its correct place, so I faced the rest of the deck. "I only meant that Alastair's techniques were impressive, and I wanted to know why his level was so different from the rest of you."

"Different or superior?" He raised an eyebrow and crossed his arms. His demeanor went from cheerful to serious. He didn't give me time to answer, though. "Al has always admired the art of sword fighting the most, so he was the one who always practiced it the most. Anyway, I am skilled enough to survive, it's quite dangerous to be a pirate."

There was something in his voice. It was almost as if he wanted to make sure he showed me his earned position as captain.

"I am aware of the dangers, I didn't say you were unskilled." As I spoke, a small smile reappeared on his lips. I liked seeing him like that. "I've always thought that the ability to sword fight would be something amazing." My eyes lowered to the weapon at his belt. "May I see it?"

"Sure." He drew it from its sheath and handed it to me.

The sword wasn't as heavy as I expected, shining in the light of the candles and hatches around the deck.

"This is beautiful! I've always wanted to hold one, but my father never allowed me to. He thought it was too dangerous."

"It can be, but I'm sure you can manage."

I felt the balance of the sword as I tilted the hilt slowly, thus shifting the entire blade to one side or the other. Although it wasn't too heavy, I couldn't imagine myself practicing with it for hours, it had already started to weigh down my outstretched arm.

"When I was a kid I used wooden swords at first, of course. Only after a certain level, I could use a real one. My arm could hardly take the weight of the steel throughout the training," he said, as if he could read my mind. I smiled and continued observing the blade, feeling his eyes on my every movement. "I could teach you how to use it if you want to."

I was so mesmerized by the weapon that my cheeks still hurt when the smile faded.

"I can't." I handed him the sword. He put it back in its sheath.

"Why not? I'm sure you could learn. If I was a disaster and now, I can survive pretty well, I'm sure you could too."

"Thanks, and I know it, but I find it hardly unlikely in only four days."

I didn't understand why his jaw dropped at my sentence, or why he nearly stuttered as he answered.

"Y-yes. Indeed, you're right. The time frame is too short to achieve such a feat."

"However, it is still enough for you to tell me more stories about your achievements. I'm curious to listen to them."

The smile returned to his face, and he began telling me of his afternoon practices with his friends back when he was a child.

After he told me some stories, Callum had his captain's duties to do and left me on the main deck. I chose to stay in his quarters for a few hours until it was time for dinner. Once again, after eating, Callum took me to the navigation room.

"Felix is not joining us tonight?" I asked once we arrived there and the red-haired man wasn't inside as I expected. He wasn't at the galley either. Callum was lighting the candles on the table.

"Oh, I've asked him and Hayden if they'd like to join us, but they declined. Apparently, they had some matters to attend to. It crossed my mind inviting Alastair, but he hardly likes anyone, so I was afraid you'd feel uneasy with his presence."

"What about Enric?"

"I knew I couldn't invite him, he's not well-behaved around pretty women and I've seen how uncomfortable he makes you feel. He tried to invite himself, though."

"And what did you tell him?"

"'You need to learn how to act towards ladies so you won't make them uncomfortable before I allow you in', those were my exact words."

I couldn't help but laugh as I imagined Enric's reaction to that. I hoped it'd have some effect on him; he was too pushy, and I believe he'd be even more so if Callum didn't have his eyes on him almost all the time.

I sat at the table. Callum did the same after getting some wine and a wooden box from the shelf Felix had put the cards in the previous day, though this one was bigger.

"Would you accept something different this time? A chess game, perhaps?"

"I'd love to. I've always been great at it."

"I'm looking forward to the challenge."

"If I can still remember it properly, it shall be fun." I grab the chess pieces and put them in place. We began the game.

Callum's honey eyes were darker and deeper in the dim light. They looked at me so attentively it was easy to distract myself. The fact that he seemed to want to talk was also not in my favor.

"You are very intriguing, Lenna."

"Why do you say that?"

"You're not only a somewhat rich girl, dressed as a commoner, you also sneaked in a pirate ship and proved to be quite resourceful."

"Resourceful?" I moved a piece that I wouldn't have moved if I were paying more attention, for he quickly took it away from the board.

"Of course. You knew valuable and privileged information earlier today. Information that no one else in this ship had, despite the fact that everyone keeps eyes and ears sharp for gossip at the docs, the kind of thing I constantly bribe people for. Yet, you were the only one who knew it and with a good amount of details."

"I was just lucky." I shrugged. "Just as I was lucky to end up in your ship. I don't know if I'd be as well treated in any other vessel as I am in here. This also makes me wonder why and how a pirate can be such a gentleman; or how the five of you are so well-educated. After all, it is rare for peasants to even read and all of you are very smart."

He moved a piece, and it was my turn to kill it easily.

"We've always had a passion for knowledge, so we pursued it. Hayden, especially."

"There is more to it."

I took another of his pieces, but I was still losing. Callum rubbed the short beard over his chin and finally settled for a challenge.

"Surprise me."

"You are pirates, but you don't attack this country. You are all from here and are still fond of it. This excludes the first idea of normal pirates that they are from the navy and rebel against their country. So I think you were formerly from the navy, which would explain your education. But something happened in the way, that maybe you wanted to take justice with your own hands. Or perhaps your families worked for privileged people, maybe even were to some extent, but something happened to them and you all decided it'd be best to live your lives at sea, which somehow led you all to rebel against the system, but not the people."

I lied down my theories, observing him with as much attention as he'd often give me. There was definitely surprise widening his eyes just a little, and then he smiled.

"You are much smarter than I gave you credit for, even if you're not half right on your assumptions."

"I'll take it as a compliment."

"That's exactly how I meant it." He moved a piece on the board. "It is indeed a delight to have such a bright woman on my ship. But alas, I have a checkmate, this time."

My eyes fell on the board; his checkmate was literal, making me lose the game.

"Indeed, you have, but I don't intend to keep it this way."

"It'd be a pity if you did."

I tried to hold on to the smile that was stubborn enough to grace my lips then. So I stood up and announced I was tired. He agreed, asking me to go ahead, and he'd return to his quarters as soon as he cleaned up the room.

Chapter Seven

Loud noises came from out of the captain's cabin. But what pushed me away from my slumber was a loud noise, almost like thunder. Callum was already up and dressed, nearly following down as the ship stirred.

"What's going on?" I sat up, balancing myself on the couch when the ship stirred to the opposite side.

"Get up." He commanded. "We're being attacked."

I stood up with difficulty and was still confused. My stomach twisted, but I held the urge to throw up the last meal on the floor. I didn't know if the sickness was coming from the moving ship or pure fright.

"I need to get you out of here."

"What? Why?"

"Because the first place they're gonna come in is my room." He grabbed my arm to help me walk through the shifting deck surface as he took me to the navigation room. "Don't leave this room." He shoved a revolver in my hands; I gasped. "Do you know how to use it?"

I shook my head.

"I've only seen guns from afar. I never even touched one before."

"Just aim and pull the trigger. Don't close your eyes doing so."

"Wait!" I grabbed his shirt the moment he turned around. My heart pounding so strongly against my chest I could hardly breathe. "You're leaving me alone here?"

"I need to go out there to help them. You'll be fine here, I promise. Lock the door and slide a shelf or the table to block the way in." He cupped my face with a hand; his touch was gentle in comparison to his serious eyes on me. "I'll be back as soon as I can."

And with that, he left the room and I didn't waste any time to lock the door. I could hear the sound of blades shocking against each other. It wasn't like before though, this time there was a less cheerful vibe to it. My whole body shivered every time gunshots crossed the air.

I wanted to know what was happening out there; I wanted to put the shelf in front of the door as he had oriented me to, but I couldn't move. Pressing my ear against the door, my imagination ran wild, and I didn't leave that spot for possibly several minutes until I broke from my stupor, knowing I had to prevent people from coming in.

I left the key and gun on the table so my now free hands could push the shelf. That thing barely moved. I put all my strength and energy into pushing it, even using my weight against the wooden furniture. But it still barely budged. It took a lot of effort for it to get even close to the door, crossing the thirty centimeters of the wall to get there. I only had to push a little more. Breathing heavily, my strained arms went numb. I never had to use them that much to move a piece of furniture this thick and heavy before.

Something collided against the door on the other

side. I instinctively covered my mouth to prevent any sound from escaping my throat, my hands shaking. More movement came from there. Two people were wrestling. My legs took me closer to the door that shook with impact again. The force was big, so probably someone threw the other person against it. Grunts escaped from both men, and when someone yelled in pain, I recognized Enric's voice.

One of Callum's friends was in peril just outside that door, and I couldn't do anything about it. I couldn't even get help. Sure, I didn't really like Enric, but they had all been so kind to me that the urge to assist him somehow was inevitable. My eyes landed on the gun on the table. Callum wouldn't have given it to me if it weren't to do something with it.

I grabbed the key and gun, unlocked the door and opened it surprisingly fast. Enric was against the wooden board and fell to the floor, I barely registered the blood on his torso and right arm; his opponent nearly fell, but kept his balance, turning to face me with raging eyes. I pointed the gun at him and shot twice, thinking of nothing else but how much I didn't want him to come closer to me. I only hit his arm as he yelled, gripping the hurt place.

I didn't know what else to do. Part of me knew I should shoot him again because he'd eventually charge against me and I would not be able to defend myself. But despite my brain screaming at my finger to press the trigger again, my body didn't obey. What if I killed him? How could I kill someone?

A hand snatched the gun from me and killed the man in my place. Enric was still sitting in the same place at the door, but that didn't stop him from shooting at other enemies coming closer. Their bodies fell against the deck near the helm, staining the floor with red.

    I was probably in shock, for I knew I was breathing, but there was not enough air for my lungs. I shook my head in an attempt to bring myself away from my numb state and quickly helped Enric stand up and enter the room. I guided him to a chair then ran to close the door. I almost had it shut when someone pushed it. I wasn't expecting it, so I was forced to step back.

    Enric didn't waste a second and was already shooting the man, however, his sight must have been blurry with blood loss for he missed his shots and soon ran out of bullets. The man saw his state and didn't mind him at all, instead; he looked at me with hungry eyes. With one swift movement, he clasped my arm, pulling me outside.

    I fought to break free from his grasp, but his big hands were too strong. He got near the taffrail, both ships were still connected by planks, but I could see each was getting ready to go their separate ways. He was trying to take me to their ship.

    I let my weight pull us down, making it hard for him to carry me away. In answer, he just used more force and hurt me more. I looked around; desperately searching for someone who could help me. Callum was fighting someone on the other side of the main deck, so I called his name at the top of my lungs. The man holding me grunted impatiently before he hit me so strongly my head spun. In my dizziness, I barely acknowledged when he got on the taffrail and started crossing the plank to his ship.

    Gunshots crossed the sky over the yells, but I couldn't tell where it came from or who was yelling. The man suddenly lost his strength, leaning on me. His body weighed me down, and I didn't even have the chance to try to keep my balance, so we both fell to the sea.

The water hit me harder than the man's hit earlier, and once again I lost my senses. There was no up and down, just the darkness surrounding me. I tried breathing, but my lungs burned causing me to choke.

Air.

I needed air, and the fact I couldn't get it into my lungs just made my heart race even more as desperation flooded inside it.

A hand surrounded my wrist and pulled me, soon an arm was around my waist. I tried to fight it but was too weak to move.

The coldness embraced me and it only made me want to sleep; the wind brushing on my wet skin. My back was against something hard. Voices sounded distant.

Something soft touched my lips then something hard pressed down my ribs and it hurt, but not as much as the salty water that seemed to rip my throat on the way out. I coughed and spit the seawater from inside, its presence still vivid within me every time I breathed.

It was a relief that the first thing I could distinguish in my blurry view was Callum's relieved smile at me. I couldn't do anything but breathe, though.

"Are you crazy?" Alastair hissed, punching the captain on the shoulder. "You could have died!"

"Stop whining, I'm fine." Callum's attention then turned back at me as he leaned closer. I was still lying on the main deck and probably all the crew was around us, but all I could see was Callum. His smooth hand found my cheek so I could look at him. His analytical eyes traced me, searching for signs of how unwell I was. "How are you?"

My throat was on fire which made it hard for me to speak. Instead, I just nodded in an attempt to show him I was conscious and fine. It worked well enough, for his expressions seemed less tense and his attention went to the surrounding people. He shouted orders and everyone began to move in a hurry. Once we were alone, he helped me sit up.

"Can you walk?"

The dizziness diminished enough for me to nod, so he helped me stand up. He guided me to his room. We were both soaked, so I didn't sit on the sofa I used as a bed, instead, I went to the chair at the small table in the middle of the room. My legs were numb and my lungs burned so much it hurt. But at least now I had precious air in and out of them.

Callum changed to dry clothes, moving faster than I could follow.

My fingers brushed against my hot cheek. The one the man had hit. It began stinging again as my senses slowly came back.

"Where are they?" I managed to ask, but my voice sounded hoarse and it failed at the end.

"They retreated once they realized they were losing." He stopped in front of me and cupped my face with a gentle touch. "I need to go out there now, you should put on some dry clothes before you catch a cold. And you need some rest, you almost drowned."

"Okay." I coughed, my throat complaining at every attempt of speaking.

"I still have some water in here for you to drink. I'll be back soon." He leaned closer and lightly kissed my forehead. The gesture was so sudden that I nearly lost my breath. Then he left the room.

Once my surprise vanished, I stood up to get rid of my wet, cold clothes.

Chapter Eight

Hours later, the sun was already shining in the sky. I was feeling much better after resting, so I left the captain's quarters to see if I could help out with something and also to check on Enric.

I helped Hayden and a middle-aged man acting like a doctor to care for the ones who were wounded. Then, I learned that they had already changed course, thus we'd reach Keanys a bit later, but safer. I also learned they had already thrown the dead at sea. They told me Enric's condition was bad, but he'd live. Hayden told me that the ship that attacked us was probably the one Enric had spotted nights ago and they somehow found us. They were indeed from Estanya's navy and they most likely recognized the ship as one of their enemies—hence the attack.

I assisted them for at least a few hours when Callum showed up looking for me. Like most people, he had an exhausted look on his face. I could tell he had been working nonstop since he woke up last night.

"I'd like to speak to you for a moment," he said.

"All right."

His hand went to my back; I believe he wasn't even

aware of it, acting without thinking.

    For a long time now, I've felt uneasy whenever a man touched me. They were usually stronger than me and I never knew what to expect from it. All I knew was I didn't want a man to touch me after getting used to uncle Oliver trying to bend me to the complying shape he wanted me to. So I was surprised when I noticed the uncomfortable shiver that would run down my spine was replaced by butterflies flying in my stomach as Callum guided me away from the infirmary.

    We went back to his room, and he closed the door.

    "Enric woke up a while ago." He pointed to a general direction behind him, probably where Enric was resting right now. "He told me what happened. What were you thinking?" Distress raised his tone.

    "I heard him on the other side of the door and I knew he was in trouble so I just acted…I know it was foolish, but I couldn't stand there doing nothing."

    "Why didn't you do as I told you and block the door?"

    "I tried, it's not my fault it was too heavy!"

    He sighed. "Of course it was…" Callum said more to himself than to me. "Still, you shouldn't have put yourself at risk. We chose this lifestyle with the dangers that came with it. We are aware of what could happen to us when we became pirates. You don't have any idea of what they would have done to you if they had kidnapped you!"

    "I'm not stupid, I know what they'd want to do with me." A shiver ran down my spine, and I embraced myself. The terror of this possibility would haunt me for the rest of my life. "I didn't think of it then."

    "You have to think of it. Always."

    I didn't let my thoughts wander that far, so I shook my head.

"After using you for their pleasure for days, they'd take you to their country and sell you to the nearest brothel they could find."

"You don't know that for sure." My stubborn side refused to believe in what he had just said.

"My crew is not as good as you think they are, I have to put a lot of effort to keep them in line! And even if they were, they'd be kind to their kind, not a foreigner. They might pretend to like us for diplomacy's sake, but that's only a façade. They don't like us and wouldn't give a fuck for you." He took a heavy breath. "Sorry, I exceeded myself..."

"It's alright. I understand."

He raised his hands to my shoulders but stopped himself before he could make contact. "I'm just glad you're safe now."

"Not more than I am." I tried to joke and it at least made him smile. Silence crept between us until I spoke. "You're right, though. I knew I wouldn't be as lucky in their ship as I was in here."

"What makes you say that?" His eyes landed on my red right cheek. He knew the answer but wanted to hear me say it.

"The way he looked at me. The way he held me. The way he hit me. I mean, I would have tried to bribe them and talk to their leader, though I don't know how well it would have worked. Of course, I haven't thought of it then."

"Reason rarely follows us when emotions dominate us."

"Indeed," I said softly.

"I'll rest for a while now. You can go help Hayden if you wish," he suggested.

"All right."

He cleared his throat. "And perhaps we could have dinner at the navigation room tonight. Games and entertainment will be a good way to relax and take our minds off of unpleasant thoughts. I'm sure that's what most people are gonna do tonight in their own way."

"Agreed. I'd love to distract myself in your company," I said and left so he could rest.

For the third night in a row after the attack, we got our dinner and headed to the navigation room. Tonight, after having our meal, we played a card game, which I won three times.

Laughing, I showed Callum the winning hand. With a frustrated smile, he put his hands on the table and started gathering them.

"I guess it's enough for tonight…I've been humiliated enough." He waved a hand in the air. "It'd be great to have you at the taverns by the harbors and win some bets."

"I'm obliged, but it was only possible because of your distractedness."

Callum shrugged and glanced at me.

"That's part of the reason."

"What do you mean?"

"Nothing in particular." He put the cards in a wooden box. "By the way, thank you."

"For what? Humiliating you?"

"No…" Callum laughed. "For making me forget how miserable I was."

"Have you drank too much? You're not making any sense."

"It's because your presence here helped me get my

mind off of how nervous I was to have to come back home. These past few days were a relief, apart from that attack a few nights ago." He sighed. "I really wish I didn't have to return."

"Are you that afraid of your brother?"

"That wouldn't be a precise word. I'm not scared of him; I just don't want to see him again. He hates me."

"Why would he do that? You're a good man!"

"Thank you, but some people have caused him to make up his mind against me and there's nothing I can do about it."

"Well, it's not fair."

"Life is rarely fair."

I wanted to say he was a pessimist, and he was wrong, but it was impossible when I'd often feel the same. Callum leaned closer and gently put a stubborn lock of hair behind my ear. It was only a simple, gentle touch that surprisingly didn't make me flinch or recoil. I didn't remember being so at ease with someone since I lost my parents.

He quickly backed away, raising his hands with a laugh. "Sorry, I forgot you don't like to be touched."

"No. It's alright. I don't mind it if it's you."

He raised an eyebrow, but his next words were playful, "What would your fiancé say if he found out about that?"

"Well, I think he'd be more shocked when I tell him I have no wish to marry him." I shrugged.

His small smile vanished; giving place to an expression that was serious and soft at the same time. In the dim light of the candles, his honey-colored eyes looked darker and deeper, drawing me in with so much intensity it was hard to look away.

"You know...we'll arrive at Keanys tomorrow." A

hand slowly reached mine and gently squeezed it.

"I know."

"So, if you prefer, we can just...set sail. I could show you the most beautiful places in this country that will take your breath away."

Was it just my imagination, or was he asking me to elope with him?

It wouldn't be a bad idea, actually. I enjoyed his company more than everyone I knew, and this lifestyle truly seemed appealing—once I learned how to defend myself properly, of course. My eyes got wet, and I resisted the urge to let the tears fall.

"I can't."

Because it'd mean my uncle would win, he'd get everything that belonged to me one way or another. I didn't want it. I couldn't let it.

"I understand..." He retrieved his hand. "Although I don't want it, I must return. I have duties to fulfill. I wouldn't be able to be away for much longer." He gulped. "But I'll be at the harbor until sunup, in case you change your mind."

Chapter Nine

I didn't imagine it'd be so hard to walk away from that ship or how difficult it would be not to look back at it once we arrived at Keanys. I'd forever be grateful for Callum and would never forget him or his kindness, but I couldn't stay. I needed to find my grandfather.

I headed to the castle. Despite my peasant clothes and years apart, aunt Sophie recognized me and let me in.

The home my mother grew up in and the place I only visited for a few times was still the way I remember it to be. The outside bore big green gardens contrasting against the gray stone of the castle walls; and as we entered, the same caramel curtains still protected the windows. The same pictures of my memories still hung on the walls with golden sconces. The soft scent of rosemary invaded my nose and went straight to my heart, lulling it with a sense of home. My mom also used rosemary perfume in my castle, and I didn't know I missed it so much until now.

Sophie was my mother's sister, and she was just as thoughtful as I remember. She took me straight to a guest room, asking some servants to bring us tea and biscuits on the way there. I was sure she'd later ask for proper clothes for me, too. She gently held my hand and led me to sit on the armchairs.

"Lia, I'm so happy to see you!" She still used the cute nickname from when I was a child, filling me with joy. She took her time to look at me, her small smile slowly turning into a frown. "But why are you here? How did you get here and why in such clothes? What happened?"

Something inside me twisted uncomfortably to bring her problems.

"I need to talk to Grandpa...he's the only one who can help me. Uncle Oliver wants me to marry the prince and thus eliminate me from the lineage of my home. I can't let him do that. Dad left his castle to me, I don't want to leave it like that and I do not wish to marry someone I don't even know!" I looked down at my peasant clothes. "I knew uncle Oliver wouldn't let me leave the castle to seek Grandpa's help, so I sneaked out one night with a servant's dress and bought a room in a navy ship."

She'd flip if she knew the truth about the ship, so I didn't feel bad lying to her this time.

"Oh, my dear." She came closer and embraced me from her armchairs. "You could have sent a letter first, you know. Or could have answered my letters. You barely answer them. In the last one I sent you a few months ago, I told you what happened with my father. He's still unwell."

"Wait, what do you mean? I haven't received a letter from you for years, now. Haven't you received mine?"

It was only after the words have left my lips that I understood what had happened. Sophie shook her head, only confirming my suspicions. Oliver was most likely intercepting my mail. Of course, he was. I'd tried asking for help before, but he wouldn't allow it, he needed me in my place so he could rule my lands as well as me.

"You don't think all those letters simply got lost, do you?" I had to shake my head.

The servants came in with a tray of drink and food, left it on the round table in front of us and left. Sophie put her hand under my chin, forcing me to look at her. "Lia, why would Oliver intercept your mail?"

"Oliver is quite controlling. I think he still needs to read the letters and tell me what's happening to protect me. He usually tells me the news from family members since he started running the lands for me when I was twelve."

"Yes, but you're nineteen now. You're a woman, not a child anymore." She clenched her fists. "I will send him a letter about it."

"No, please don't trouble yourself any further, aunt Sophie. I will do this myself."

"We'll see about that. I'll give you a month to start receiving your letters back and not a day more. If I don't receive one from you by then, my husband and I'll go there in person."

I did my best to smile, but I knew it wouldn't change anything. They couldn't do anything against Oliver. Plus most of the servants were loyal to him, not me. He had the upper hand on the situation. They also couldn't take Oliver away from my lands; it was his family's, after all. However, Grandpa had always had this way of making people do as he wished. He knew how to persuade people, he was imposing, powerful and he knew how to turn the tables in his favor. I was sure he could come up with some deal Oliver would have to take and then leave me alone. Although Grandpa was from my mother's side, Oliver usually respected the elderly, at least to some extent, and especially if they were powerful figures.

I held my aunt's hand.

"What happened with grandpa?"

Sophie sighed and began to tell me the events.

Grandpa had tripped and fallen several months ago causing him to break his leg. It wasn't completely healing; doctors said due to his old age, it was unlikely to heal properly, so he was trapped in his bed. The days left alone there aggravated his depression after Grandma passed away a few years ago. Now, he was barely sane. Sophie had sent me letters about it, but I hadn't received them.

As I entered his room to visit I was met with him smiling. He said how much I reminded him of his wife, in the middle of the conversation, he even called me by her name. I stayed by his side for hours with a dreadful feeling I wouldn't see him alive after I returned home.

Once again, Sophie volunteered to come back to talk to uncle Oliver, but it'd be useless, so I declined. He'd punish me for trying to ask for help, and just the thought of it made me shiver.

I had no way out of that situation.

At night, I laid in bed, staring at the ceiling for hours, too numb to do anything else but breathe, unable to sleep.

"I'll be at the harbor until sunup..." Callum's words invaded my mind.

My heart vibrated with a small wave of hope that compelled me to stand up and put on my peasant clothes again. It wasn't ideal, and I didn't want Oliver to get anything from me anyway, but at least I'd be free to do whatever I wanted. I'd be free to marry whoever and whenever I wanted, if it was my desire.

I left the castle unseen by the guards, I barely even thought about it and would have to send a letter to Sophie later. I ran to the harbor. It was a long way as I crossed the deserted streets and went straight to where the ship had docked...however; the place was empty. A man working at the harbor whistled a song nearby, and I went to him.

"Excuse me, have you seen a galleon ship docked right there earlier today?"

"Oh, dear...you're too late. It set sail moments ago." He pointed at the horizon.

As the sky turned orange as dawn broke, the silhouette of a big ship heading towards the open sea became more visible. Callum hadn't kept his word, and thus the remaining unbroken piece of my heart shattered down.

Chapter Ten

It took me almost two weeks to get back to my castle. Oliver was infuriated and took me straight to the king's palace to meet my fiancé. He threw me in his carriage, then we left. During the days we spent on the way, we stopped at his friend's castles and houses, where he locked me in a room so I wouldn't run away again. Though I wasn't going anywhere, there was no place to go. My chance of escaping had slipped through my fingers.

The royal palace was bigger than mine, however, the Queen-mother needed the wealth from my lands; to do so, she and Oliver made an agreement to marry her youngest son. Of course, I had no say in it.

Rumors say the king couldn't have children, so that was why the Queen wanted to marry her youngest son to ensure the crown's offspring; Oliver liked to know about it.

Alone in the corridors, I stopped to observe the paintings on the wall, pictures of old kings and queens. There was one of our actual kings, sitting at the throne. As far as I knew, he had lost the ability to walk, but soon I found another one, which he stood in an imposing pose.

"It's time to meet your dearest future husband." Oliver's voice reached my ears. He grabbed my elbow harshly and pulled me down the hall. "You will be the perfect lady and stay quiet."

He wished! But I was not going to accept it like that. As if he could read my mind, he pulled me to the side to face him.

"I am serious. I've been your guardian for all these years and I know what's best for you so you *will* obey me." I wanted to laugh, but I remained silent. I guess he saw the defiance in my eyes. This was hard to contain. He didn't like it, and before I could even blink, his very heavy hand landed loudly on my cheek. My face burned in pain and I let out a startled little gasp as my eyes got wet. "Behave accordingly. Don't make me correct you again."

I shivered. I still had bruises from his 'correction' when I returned home.

With a smile, he put a strand of hair back into my bun. Grabbing my hand, he put it around his arm and forced me not to move as he kept a hand on mine. He was ready to pinch me if I said anything wrong, and I hated it when he did that. I looked down and let him push me to the throne-room.

The Queen was sitting there but stood up to greet us. I barely looked at her, but I hoped I could find a way to talk to her alone later and explain the situation. Surely I could convince her to stop this insanity, even if I had to give her some wealth, the lands were mine, after all; not Oliver's. I just needed a few moments with her. I was sure Oliver would do his best for it not to happen, though.

"I'm delighted to meet you at last!" She told me and I bowed. "You are as beautiful as your mother, just as your uncle claimed you to be."

"I'm obliged, your Majesty."

I glanced at her, then my focus went back to the floor. She gestured for someone to get closer.

"My youngest boy was away for a long time, but he has returned on time for this meeting. I knew he would, he always keeps his word."

Someone stopped in front of me, but I wasn't ready to lift my head, until I heard a familiar voice softly whispering, "Lenna…"

My jaw dropped. Standing right in front of me was a person I thought I'd never see again, though this time his clothes were different, and he had shaved. His wide eyes were as surprised as mine.

"Callum." I whispered, but Oliver immediately pinched me. I couldn't call our prince by the first name if I didn't know him.

The Queen laughed at her son, probably thinking he had mistaken me for someone else. She hadn't noticed what Oliver had just done, but I couldn't say the same for Callum. His sharp honey-colored eyes that landed on my hand and then on my reddish cheek.

"No, my dear," the Queen said. "This is Amelia Leannain, your fiancée."

He was successful in containing his surprise.

"About that, Mother, I'd like to have a moment with her and show her the garden."

The Queen agreed. But before I could even think of saying anything, Oliver squeezed my hand so tightly I nearly yelped.

"I don't think it's a good idea, my niece is fairly shy and reserved."

Callum smiled, triumphantly. "Please. I insist."

He extended his arm to me and it'd be rude if I didn't accept the gesture, even if I didn't want to. Which was not the case, so I immediately forced my hand away from his grasp and grabbed Callum's arm. He was quick in leading me outside and only when we were away from prying ears, he spoke freely.

"I thought you were just rich, not the richest person in the realm! You are richer than me! Your lands not only provide food for a third of the realm, but also has the biggest mine of gold!"

"Yes, I am aware of *my* profits." I finally let go of his arm. "And I didn't know your brother was the king! And I don't understand, I thought he was sick, why hadn't you returned home earlier?"

"That's exactly why I had to leave. When we were young, he got some sort of sickness and lost the ability to move his legs. When Father died and he was crowned. There were some people that believed he couldn't properly fulfill his role as a ruler because of that and wanted me to be crowned. Arguments got worse to a point he believed I was plotting against him, even if I wasn't. So leaving was the best option I had at the time. Part of the reason for this marriage was because my mother wanted to force me to return."

"And because you need more wealth."

"Of course."

"And so you left to become a pirate."

"Not exactly. I left with some loyal friends and servants, but we stayed for a few years in one of my castles in the north. However, we got bored, and we had the idea to set sail. All agreed, I got a ship and headed to the seas. First, we acted as a trading ship, but when word came to me that there was a country messing up with the agreements with my country, we decided to steal from them, thus we became pirates."

He laughed and stopped in the middle of the garden. His hand slowly reached my cheek in a soft touch, his expression already completely changed in an instant, showing how serious he was.

"But I'm sorry about this." He retrieved his hand and cleared his throat. "Anyway, we can arrange another agreement for the wedding and I'll make sure he won't hurt you again."

"Good, because I have no wish to marry a liar."

"What do you mean? I've kept my word to you!"

"You didn't!" In a lush of anger, I hit him on the chest, though luckily, the guards didn't seem to notice I had hit their prince. "You said you'd be there until sunrise, but when I got there just before then, you had already left! I crossed the streets at night, alone, and frightened for nothing because you had set sail minutes before you said you would! You abandoned me, you liar!"

Callum reached for my hands. "So you came back to me?"

"Are you deaf or stupid? That's what I said!"

His face lit up in silly hope in those lips that curved into a smile.

"I had stood there the entire day, looking at the harbor, praying to see you again, but you didn't even look back...my friend convinced me to depart a little earlier."

"If you hadn't listened to him, you'd have kept your private entertainment on board. Now that we're here, I just need your assistance to get my uncle away from me and I will provide your mom with what she needs."

"Wait!" He prevented me from walking away, still holding my hands. "You had chosen me, let me redeem myself to you."

"I had chosen a pirate, not a prince. And he broke my

heart."

"Then give this prince a chance, he won't make the same mistake." In a gentle motion, he guided my hands up so he could kiss mine.

I couldn't deny I felt something warm inside me, almost as if the shattered pieces of my heart were ready to mend. I liked his company and admired his character, being married to him didn't seem like a bad idea, in fact, I found myself wanting more of him as I got lost in his honey eyes.

I stepped closer until his breath brushed my skin. I kissed him, and Callum let go of my hands to pull me in. I caught myself doing the same as my hands surrounded his neck and I couldn't deny anymore: I wanted him.

Epilogue

Just because I wanted Callum, it didn't mean it'd be easy for him. He had to earn my heart and prove to me he deserved it. He assured me he had a plan and three days later, at the ball for the official announcement of our wedding, he'd put it into action. I had to admit; I was quite curious.

The Queen provided me a new dress for the ball since my options were limited by the ones I'd brought. So I entered the Great Hall in a sapphire gown, adorned in golden details, covered in jewelry. I could feel everyone's eyes on me, but I couldn't decide if it was positive or negative.

The King was sitting on the throne, overlooking the ballroom as five steps elevated the place where the thrones were. It was the first time I've seen him. He resembled his younger brother, though the much longer beard and tired brown eyes made him look even older than he truly was. He was so lean he didn't seem healthy enough, which made the rumors of his weakness truer.

The Queen was sitting by his left side and Callum was sitting on the other side. His dazzling honey orbs scanned the ballroom in a serious and thoughtful expression up until the moment he found me. A small smile appeared, and even from afar I could see a gleam in his eyes.

I looked at my uncle on the other side of the room as if urging Callum to go on with his plan. He nodded slowly, acknowledging my silent request, but also lifted up a hand discreetly as if asking me to wait. He pointed at my uncle, and I followed the direction. I was surprised as I realized the red-haired man by Oliver's side, pouring wine in his cup, was Felix.

So I waited.

When it was time for the official announcement, the King declared his mother was to do the formalities; the Queen stood up and proceeded to explain the joyous occasion, gesturing for me to come closer. I walked up to her as she told the nobles in the room about the future wedding. That was when Callum stood up.

"It was a surprise to me when I received a letter from my mother about it, but now I admit I couldn't be happier with her choice." He held my hand and kissed it lightly. "And I also must admit I was astounded to know about my wonderful fiancée's past. I shall thank Duke Oliver Leannain for raising her and taking care of her lands after her parents passed away. A marvelous deed, indeed."

I squeezed his hand. Was he out of his mind?

He ignored my glares and continued with a smile on his face as my uncle dismissed it, humbly.

"It was my duty, your Royal Highness." His voice was slurred and relaxed, I knew he had had too much wine in his system already.

"It certainly was, but I've heard of your work there. In fact, I'm so admired by it that I want to personally invite you to take care of the crown's finances. I'm sure our team is competent enough, but it'd be an honor to have this brilliant addition working for King."

As if on cue, Hayden, standing by Oliver's side, exclaimed in awe, almost too exaggerated, putting a hand on my uncle's shoulder and congratulating him before he could even think of an answer. Enric soon began clapping and was followed by the rest of the nobles. Oliver tried to say something, but his voice was almost inaudible by the clapping; once it was over, Callum declared he was happy with his approval and now Oliver couldn't decline the job.

It couldn't be a coincidence; they had set it up.

The sharp stare the Queen gave to Callum told me she wasn't aware of it.

"Now, I believe it's time for our first dance." Then the Prince guided me to the center of the hall, people already moving out of our way, leaving the center only for both of us as the music started playing again.

He put his free hand on my back and glided around in the rhythm of the song, almost tripping here and there, nearly as rusty at dancing as I was.

"What were you thinking?" I hissed.

"My dear Lenna, I want my enemies close as much as I want my friends."

"But he'll be right here all the time."

"You wanted him out of your lands and I did it. My friends will make sure his acceptance to it will be the talk of the night and tomorrow morning. He won't be able to decline. And those who work for the crown receive power and prestige, however, they must not have lands of their own."

Which was why only nobles who had no right to heir anything ended up working for the crown.

"Yes, but I also didn't want him here. Besides, now everything that is supposed to be mine will go to his son, which is just as bad."

"But until we marry, your lands will be yours. You'll be in charge of them for the next few months, you can even appoint a family successor since you don't have any heirs. It would of course, naturally be your cousin's but I'm sure we can work something out until the wedding. Any good excuse, the support of the Queen and Prince should be enough to send your lands straight to whomever you like."

That was something I didn't expect, and that I liked even more than I could have imagined. I had to admit, his plan was brilliant, but he didn't stop there.

"Besides, here, I'll keep an eye on him and Hayden will keep an eye on his work. If we catch him doing anything wrong to you or my brother's money, we can send him straight to the dungeon."

I liked this part even more. My greedy uncle would attempt to steal before the first month was over. He'd be arrested before the wedding and I would never have to see him again.

"Well, my cousin has a younger sister. She had always been nice and I think she could make good use of my lands, but she's too young."

"Once we arrest your uncle, we can pressure your cousin to leave your land to clean their names by working for the crown on his father's place. That'll leave the younger cousin in charge, but Hayden can help her until she's at age."

Callum has kept his word, and I liked his plan so much it was hard to contain my smile.

"I guess you approve of my plan?"

"You are smarter than I gave you credit for."

"My friends helped me with some details. It was Felix's idea to make Oliver drink more than he should so he wouldn't have time to deny my proposal."

"Thanks."

"Have I passed the test?"

"So far, yes."

Callum totally ignored the protocol when he leaned to kiss me in front of everyone. It was quick, though. He had proved to me he would keep his word. I believed he would take my broken heart and take care of it, maybe even better than I had done.

Acknowledgments

Since I can't do everything by myself, this story wouldn't have set sail if there weren't for some very important people in my life. So thank you to:

To my parents, Ana Maria and Eduardo Barbosa, for shaping my character through the hard work of raising me.

To my dear high school friend and beta of everything I write, Nathally Simonetti, thanks for helping and supporting me for so long!

To my long-time friend, Rebeca Kelmer, who has always helped and supported me in my writing journey.

To my friend Diego Pessoa, for always helping me with my biology questions when I need to hurt one of my characters.

To my dear beta reader friends who helped me improve this story: Indrė Lionikaitė; Débora Silva; and Susana Silva!

And to my editor, Faith Lane, for all the corrections and details I needed to do to make it on point.

About the Author

Born and raised in Brasilia (Brazil), Marília Barbosa is the oldest of three sisters and graduated in Design and Japanese, but is also graduating in English. Living with her head in the clouds, she fell in love with creating stories at 14, when she started playing and creating stories with her friends at school. With time, she took the writing more seriously and now it takes all the author's free time that by every story she finishes, she has already five new ones in her mind.

You can find her on:
Instagram: @author.marilia
Wattpad: https://www.wattpad.com/user/MariliaGB

Other books available on Amazon and Wattpad:

Between the Land and the Sea (YA contemporary supernatural romance, short story)

Thor, the Cat (YA contemporary romance, short story)

Thor's First Christmas (YA contemporary romance, short story)

Valentine's Day Under the Stars (YA contemporary romance, short story)

The Night of the Last Disappearance (contemporary supernatural suspense, short story)

A Tale of Blood and Flames (fantasy romance, short story)

The Duchess at Sea (historical romance, novella)

**Thank you so much for reading!
If you enjoyed this short story, please leave a review and spread the word in social media.**

Turn the page for a small gift. Since "The Duchess at Sea" is just a novella, I added two short stories for your enjoyment in this paperback version.

The short stories below and many others are also available as eBooks on Amazon.

The extra short stories you have next are:

Valentines Day Under the Stars
(Contemporary Romance)
Summary: After receiving yet another prank letter on Valentine's Day, Sarah decides to erase the date on her calendar, but her best friend doesn't think the same way.

Between the Land and the Sea
(Contemporary Supernatural Romance)
Summary: Iara had the habit of walking down the beach almost every afternoon, picking up trash from the sand as volunteer work, until a weird boy shows up and lurks around her. When she decides to confront him so he stops bothering her, she ends up finding out his huge secret.

Enjoy the reading!

Marília G Barbosa

VALENTINE'S
one letter
DAY UNDER
one love
THE STARS
one chance

Valentine's Day Under the Stars

I clenched the heart-shaped letter in my shaky hands. I thought getting out of high school meant I wouldn't receive any more of these ridiculous, meaningless letters. But no. I guess everywhere it is possible to find stupid people, doing stupid things, messing around with other people's feelings.

Looking around the classroom, I tried to determine which classmate could have done this; during middle and high school, I eventually learned of the ones who would mess around with me once a year. Now, however, I was starting from scratch.

Most of the students seemed to actually be concentrating on answering the question the teacher had asked them. However, I knew Ms. Gomez would eventually let us finish it at home and I could properly concentrate there. I held back the urge to complain out loud, but a whimper must have escaped my lips since Leila, sitting by my side, put a gentle hand on my shoulder and scooted closer.

"Are you okay?" Her azure eyes blinking in concern but also curiosity at me.

I breathed heavily in an attempt to calm myself down.

"Yes...I just hate this time of the year." I shrugged and leaned on my desk as soon as I hid the heart-shaped letter under my notebook.

"What do you have against Valentine's Day, Sarah?" Owen's voice was low and quiet behind me. I had figured he'd been listening, he was more of a curious person than I was. Both Leila and Owen had been my first friends when I entered college. I was so glad I met them, I wouldn't have known how to navigate this whole new world without them. "It's just a special day to spend with people we love."

I turned to face him, meeting his adorable, puppy dog-like, caramel eyes. My heart always beats quicker when I see them, enough to make me sigh and I have to try to get it back to normal.

"Yes, but we should always do that no matter the day. Maybe not every day, but often, that's for sure. It's stupid to think people can have a special day like this once a year."

"You do know people *do* go out throughout the year too, right?" Leila joked, trying to lighten up the mood—like she always did.

"I know, but today is just a silly commercial day, only meant to sell flowers, heart-shaped letters, heart-shaped chocolates in heart-shaped boxes and heart-shaped everything! It's ridiculous, really." I twirled a lock of dark curly hair in my copper tanned fingers, trying to relax. "It's nothing but an excuse to make people buy and sell things they don't really need, it's all for capitalism."

"You can't complain of capitalism while wasting half your savings on gadgets and collectible fandom figures on sale every Black Friday," Owen pointed out.

I glared at him.

"That's totally different, I need those things. I don't, however, need heart-shaped chocolate," I huffed. "Squares, cubes or circles are just fine."

Owen shrank in his desk. I didn't even look up to see if Professor Gomez was looking at us, I just shut up, looking at the list of exercises and pretended to be writing in my notebook for a while. I knew I should be studying, but my brain just stopped working when I found that letter in my backpack, and now, the red edge of it was lurking under my notebook as if taunting me with its presence. I needed to get rid of it.

"So, who was the guy?" Leila asked me in a whisper.

"What guy?"

"The one who broke your heart. You're too bitter to blame only the selling of 'useless' products. So, who is he?"

"Surprisingly enough, I've never had a guy break my heart like that," I sighed. Grabbing the letter under my notebook, I shoved it into her hands. "I'm just tired of pranks like these!"

It hurt to have had received so many letters from classmates that only wanted to toy with my feelings. They made me hopeful and happy, even made me feel special to be admired for getting Valentine's cards, only to find out they were nothing but a lie. It started off as one event with them laughing behind my back, but then it became a yearly event to break my heart over and over.

Leila opened the heart and read its contents, meanwhile, Owen stared at it, and I could only imagine he was trying to figure out what was written in it. He turned to me.

"What's up with it?" His voice sounded even lower now and I tried not to get distracted at the way his tousled dark locks fell around his face. It was the perfect kind of messy, not too much but not too little. It was like he woke up and adjusted it with his fingers, looking effortlessly stunning.

"This is so sweet!" Leila gave me back the letter, her voice also going down as she looked around to see if we got anyone's attention with our little chat. I didn't really care anymore, this was college, not high school; therefore it's not like we would be sent to the principal.

"It's not sweet. Not sweet at all."

"Why not? You got a secret admirer who has liked you since you started college."

"That's the point. Why not tell that to my face? Why hide? It's because this person is just fooling around. It's nothing but a prank." I ripped the letter in half. Both Leila and Owen's eyes widened at the red paper pieces; his cheeks lightly flushed, but I didn't know why. "If it were true, the person would have the decency to sign it. Or tell me face to face. No one here is a child." I looked around the room again, wondering who had given me the card. I needed to do something about it to stop this prank before it became another yearly tradition.

"Or maybe the person was too shy to sign?" Leila suggested.

"Maybe, but in my experience, signing or not, it was never real and I'm sick of it!" I crossed my arms. "Do you know who could have done it?" I gave her back one piece and Owen the other. "Do you guys recognize the handwriting? It's pretty."

"No, sorry," Leila said as Owen frowned and shook his head. They gave me back the pieces.

"Okay. It doesn't matter. If I find this person, the prankster will pay for this prank."

The rest of the classes went by rather slowly since I couldn't focus on the subjects. Owen was unusually quiet while Leila tried to distract me throughout the classes we had together, which was most of them. And finally, it was time to go home.

In need of a change of thought that didn't have to do with the dreaded holiday or college, I put it all aside to watch a bloody medieval fantasy TV show.

After three and a half episodes, my phone rang, bringing me back to reality. I paused the show and reached for the noisy device, answering it after checking the caller ID.

"Hey, Owen, what's up?"

"Hi, Sarah, don't you look at your messages anymore?" He chuckled.

"Sorry, I was watching TV and didn't see them…"

"That's okay. You know, I was thinking about what you said earlier and you're right."

"About what? Valentine's Day is a waste of time?"

"No. That we shouldn't spend only one day of the year with the people we appreciate and like, we should do this every time we want and I think maybe we could go out to do something. Just because we're friends, doesn't mean we can't do this, right?"

"I guess, but I don't think I'm in the mood today, sorry."

"Well, today might be Valentine's, but it's just a day like any other. Come on, I think you need to get your head off of things and just have some fun. I promise you won't regret it," he insisted a little bit more. I wanted to go out with him, geez, I had a crush on him the first time I laid eyes on him and the feeling just grew as I got to know the amazing person he is…however, I was so annoyed I'd probably just bore him away. I sighed, but before I could say anything, he continued. "I promise there won't be any flowers or heart-shaped chocolate, just your regular favorite chocolate bar. Please don't say no, because I don't wanna return dad's car so soon..."

"Return dad's car?" Something in the back of my mind screamed to go to the window. It was almost like he wanted to hint that he was there, but it couldn't be...there he was, in the parking lot, leaning on his dad's car. My jaw dropped.

"So, what do you say? Let's have some fun? I mean, we usually like to stay indoors and all, but maybe today we could do something different." He shrugged.

"I...I'm not ready." I knew it was something stupid to say, but I could barely think.

"It's okay, I have a book, just don't leave me hanging for too long."

"Well, alright then. After all, it's not every day your dad lets you use his car." I laughed and ended the call, still shocked Owen was allowed to borrow it since his dad was so strict towards it.

Next thing I knew, I had thrown half my wardrobe on my bed so I could quickly find something nice to wear. I settled for my best jeans, a cute black blouse with printed flowers, a necklace, and beige moccasins. Luckily, my hair wasn't too dirty, so I pulled it into a half-bun, leaving only part of the curly locks loose. I put on my shoes and I left the apartment I shared with other college students and met him outside. Owen was patiently reading in the driver's seat, he threw the book in the backseat and unlocked the doors so I could get in.

"You look...wonderful," he nearly stuttered as I sat down and closed the door.

"Thanks. You don't look bad yourself."

I took a minute to see him up close, his worn-out jeans were replaced for new black ones, paired with a nice button-down navy blue shirt that I didn't even know he had and black Allstars. His short messy locks seemed to have been brushed, something he had confessed barely doing. His brown eyes—like melted chocolate—gleamed in joy as he smiled at me and then revived the engine.

"So, where are we going?" I asked.

"You'll see."

The mystery and playfulness in his voice made my heart flutter and I couldn't help but smile even more. He drove away and I tried to guess where he was going, but could only know when the circular building shape of the Planetarium came into view.

He entered the parking lot and I waited until the car was safely in a spot to turn to him.

"You remembered!"

"Of course." He shrugged as he turned off the engine. "You wanted to come here for a while, but every time we're going out with our friends we end up going somewhere else."

"And when we plan to come here something has to get in our way. I haven't been here since my parents brought my sisters and me when we were kids," I said.

"I haven't come here for a few years either. I guess we usually just forget about its existence. I certainly did until you started talking about it." He opened his door, so I did the same, and we both got out of the car.

We walked along the path to the building, greeted by a cool gentle breeze and the warm sunlight of the end of the afternoon. There were some people with children around the Planetarium, but also many couples, after all, it was Valentine's Day, so of course people would be celebrating it.

My stomach twisted as I glanced at Owen by my side. Were people thinking we were a couple, too? We were just friends and nothing else, but I couldn't help but feel my heart fill with hope and anxiety.

I pushed away those thoughts and forced myself to concentrate on the exhibits we wanted to see. There was only a café, lockers and the reception, so we asked for information and then we went up to the second floor to begin our tour. I found planetariums to be fascinating, and I also wasn't the kind of girl to be found at parties and bars. I preferred museums. As we exited the elevator, we were met with some meteorites, pieces and stones from outer space, followed by big panels of stunning pictures from stars, nebulas, galaxies, and more.

My jaw dropped in awe as I stepped closer to one of the biggest pictures of a nebula, which was a colored mist with many shades of blue, purple and pink, covered in bright white and yellow dots.

"This is so amazing! I wonder if it's all real or if they're only simulations."

"Well, it says it's from a satellite," Owen answered, looking at the small text under the picture. "And it seems like this is where stars are born."

"That's cute!" I smiled. "But these babies are probably older than humanity."

"Well, you know, just a few millions of years, nothing much." He shrugged playfully and we both laughed, resuming our walk.

This part of the exhibition finished so we went up to the third floor. There was a small exhibit of the time the U.S. and Russia were racing to reach the moon and a white spacesuit to demonstrate what it looks like. On the rest of the floor, there was a circular room where we entered to see some short educational movies.

The screen was the entire semi-circle ceiling, there was a big projector in the center and many chairs in circular rows. I didn't remember it was so big, so as I got distracted, Owen grabbed my hand to guide me to a chair. I almost sank in the fluffy cushion and leaned backward.

"I think it's bigger than I remember."

"No, it's not," He chuckled.

"How do you know that?"

"I did my research before I picked you up. Remember it was closed for a few years?" I nodded in response. "Before they reopened it, they did some restorations and improved this room, using its space better. The only change was that they replaced the old chairs for these new recliners so we can watch more comfortably."

I didn't have the words to express how touched I was to know he really took an effort for this date. No, it wasn't a date. I had to remind myself that this wonderful, funny, gentle eighteen-year-old man was a friend. Just a friend. This was only a friendly night out and he was only trying to make me feel better because he was my *friend*.

Though when the lights went out to begin the show, I didn't miss the fact that his hand was still in mine. He didn't seem to notice it, though. Part of me wanted to fool myself into believing he could return my feelings, but as always, my rational part quickly smashed the false hope and forced my focus on the movie. Luckily, it wasn't very hard as the images were so fascinating as they explained years of studying planets, moons, eclipses, and stars in about forty minutes. Schools should definitely have more field trips here.

"Well, now, should we get something to eat?" he

asked, letting go of my hand as we stood up and exited the room. I gave my best normal smile, hoping my face wasn't as red, as it still felt warm.

"Sure!"

We took the elevator to the first floor again and headed to the café we had seen when we came in. I ordered a cappuccino and an apple pie while he ordered a cup of hot chocolate and a quiche slice.

"So, how did you convince your dad to use the car?" Owen's dad loved his car, after all.

"It wasn't that hard, he just wasn't gonna use it tonight. He actually liked the idea, cause now he and my mom have the house all to themselves for at least a couple of hours."

"Let me guess, your brother went out with his girlfriend for Valentine's Day."

"Fiancée." He smiled as he sipped his hot chocolate.

My jaw dropped, luckily it was right before I put some food in my mouth and not after. I knew both Owen and his brother chose college closer to home and his brother still lived with his parents to save up money to ask his girlfriend, but I didn't expect it to be so soon, the couple graduated months ago.

"What? Already?"

"If she says yes by the end of the evening, yes."

"Congratulations to him!" I said as soon as I swallowed.

"I'll let him know."

Soon—sooner than I liked—, we finished eating, I wanted to split the bill, but he refused and paid before I could try to do anything about it. Then we headed back to the car in slow steps. He was probably just following my pace, but I was willingly taking as long as I could to enjoy a few more moments. It didn't really work, because it seemed like a blink of an eye and we were already back in my parking lot. Surely it wasn't this fast for real, the ride was so nice it just went by smoothly like that...anyway, where did the time go?

"Well..." he sighed. "Here we are."

"Yes. I guess I should go, then. Thanks, by the way. It was very fun to go out with you."

"I'm glad to hear that." Although he smiled, his paused tone suggested he was rather nervous.

"See you in class tomorrow."

My hand reached the car handle and opened the door, but before I could exit, Owen gulped and when he spoke, his voice came out quite shaky.

"I've looked at you since the first day you stepped in. You're smart, beautiful and sincere. You're too amazing for me, but I wish I could be yours."

My eyes widened and I closed the door again, turning to face him.

"How do you know what was written if you didn't read it?" Then everything clicked and my voice almost failed in surprise. "Unless you were the one who wrote it!"

"I didn't mean it as a joke!" He quickly explained. He cleared his throat. "I didn't know how to tell it and it seemed like a good way, I didn't know you've been pranked before. I'm so sorry...I didn't mean to upset you."

"But...that definitely wasn't your handwriting."

"Yes, of course not, I can barely read my own handwriting. So I asked my brother to write down what I wanted in the letter."

I was stunned. I didn't know what to do or think, and I think he felt the same because he was so red his face could easily pass as a giant tomato. I was lucky that my skin was a few shades darker than his so I couldn't be that red, although it certainly felt like I was...

I opened my mouth a few times before I could mumble a coherent sentence.

"So you meant that for real?"

"Yes, I'm sorry I couldn't tell it before or sign the letter. I didn't have the courage." He gulped yet again and then his voice came out in a whisper. "I'll understand if you just don't want to talk about it again. We can just forget this date and pretend it never happened."

Oh, I was not willing to go back like before now that I knew he liked me, even if just a bit more than simply a friend. After all, I hardly doubt he'd give the letter to me on Valentine's Day if he didn't like me as a possible girlfriend.

The letter I despised and ripped apart right in front of him.

"I-I'm so sorry! I didn't know the letter was yours! And I just sliced it in two..."

"It's okay. It was my fault. I shouldn't have sent it to you in the first place."

Now he was making that innocent-guilty face, almost like a dog who has done something wrong. It was quite adorable, as always.

"I don't think I want to go back to the way it was before. And I wouldn't have ripped the letter apart if it was signed because..." I sighed, my heart raced so fast I could barely breathe. "Because I feel the same way towards you."

He was so surprised, he turned to face me as if I had just told him I had two heads.

"Wait, you do?"

I leaned closer and kissed him. It was quick and short, it's not like I had experience in this kind of stuff; I'm used to being mocked on Valentine's, not admired or asked out. I was just a nerd that guys wouldn't consider even for the last option. At least not until today.

He was frozen, maybe he was out of practice for as long as I have. Once the shock wore out, he leaned closer to meet my lips for a second time. The kiss lasted longer now as he put an arm around me, pushing me closer and the other hand on my cheek. A warm tingly sensation filled me like a hot air balloon and I felt like I was floating, so I held him tighter.

"So...should we repeat today's experience, then?" He asked in a shy tone.

"Yes, hopefully not next Valentine's Day?" I attempted to lighten up the mood with a joke so my heart could take the time to calm down.

"I was thinking about on Saturday."

"Sure. I'd love it."

"Great! I know a nice restaurant I'm sure you'll love."

"I'm already looking forward to it."

I leaned in for another kiss and then left the car. My head was spinning and I still felt like it was a dream or hallucination; maybe there was some sort of drug in the pie I ate or the coffee I drank. It proved to be true, however, when later that night, Owen texted me, saying how happy he was to meet me for our first official date on Saturday.

I guess Valentine's Day wasn't going to be so bad anymore.

BETWEEN THE LAND AND THE SEA

MARÍLIA G. BARBOSA

Between the Land and the Sea

The rough and warm sand of the beach was in perfect contrast to the constant wind. Iara took a deep breath, smelling the scent of the sea, put on her headphones, pressed play on her phone, and then started her walk.

As usual, Iara carried her flip-flops between her fingers to enhance the feeling of the ocean waves as they reached the sand. Her dark hair, which was just like her native Brazilian mom's, was braided to the side; her milk chocolate skin shining in the sun while she enjoyed another late afternoon with that beautiful view as far as the eye could see.

However, before the first song on her playlist even ended, an empty and partially covered by sand plastic bottle appeared on her way. It was amazing how people seemed incapable of picking up their own trash and properly disposing of it as they left. That had happened so many times before that now Iara always had a trash bag in her pocket, so she picked up other pieces of trash she could find on her way.

Plastic bottles, beer and soda cans, cigarette butts, plastic cups, bags and wraps.

She found so many things daily that it was hard to believe she lived in a civilized world. As she strode towards the end of her walk, the weight in her hand disappeared with the sound of plastic softly hitting the sand.

She let out a groan of frustration and bent down to pick everything up all over again. Without a backup bag, she was forced to try and gather it all in her hands to take it to the nearest trash can. Before she realized it, one of the many plastic bottles rolled down the sand until it reached the ocean and floated away; that is, until someone grabbed it and threw it back to Iara, hitting her in the back with it.

Dropping everything on the sand, the enraged girl stood up and scanned the direction from which the projectile had come, finding nothing but a boy in the ocean, staring at her not too far from where she was.

"Hey, you!" she yelled, not caring about the curious looks she got from the people around her. "Do you think throwing bottles at people is funny? Littering on the beach too? You know it can take centuries for one of these to be decomposed by nature? Why is it so hard for some people to simply look for a trash can to throw their trash in?"

She wrapped up her little speech looking at the people around her. Surprised, the boy was speechless, opening and closing his mouth like a fish until he decided to dive in and swim away.

She clicked her tongue and bent down once again to pick up the trash and take it to its righteous place. She had to make two trips to get rid of everything she had picked up before. When she was finally finished, Iara went home, waiting to tell her cousin—who she shared her tiny and simple apartment with—all about it and have fun with Isabella's reaction.

Iara went back to the beach almost every day that week, always in the late afternoon, after her shift at the clothing store.

Usually, she didn't pay attention to whoever was at the beach, except for the boy who had thrown the bottle at her, but just because he was super weird. For starters, he was so pale it looked like he had never seen the sun, and he was always in the ocean, far away from the people. Besides that, he kept staring at her, and that pissed Iara off. She even thought about confronting him, but he never left the water. Not even after the night had fallen and she was sure the water was very cold since no one else could stand being in it. So, she went home, because she had to wake up early the next morning either way.

However, on Sunday, everything was going to be different. On her day off, she went to the beach at the usual time, in the late afternoon, and, once again, the boy was there.

As always, Iara pretended to ignore him and went on her walk, throwing away the garbage she found on her way. This time, however, she went down to a kind of isolated area of the beach, which had tons of brown rocks that reached into the sea.

It wasn't recommended to go up the rocks since they were slippery, but that didn't stop her, still holding her flip-flops in one hand. And as she expected, the boy was subtly following her.

"Hey, you, little fish!"

He slowly approached her, looking around with a suspicious look on his face. There were some people nearby, who curiously watched, while others just ignored them and carried on with whatever they were doing.

"Little fish?"

"Well, of course! You never leave the water!" She put her hands on her waist, raising her voice to the fullest. "What is the matter with you? Why do you keep following me?"

The boy's voice was still low like he wanted no one else but her to listen to him.

"You don't pollute the sea."

Iara had no reaction for a few moments.

"Yeah..." She shrugged. "And?"

"I don't understand. I thought everyone did that."

She was still confused but ended up laughing.

"Are you out of your mind? Of course, there are tons of people doing what they are not supposed to, but it's not like that! There are also people who are worried about the environment, alright?"

"Really? 'Cause it doesn't seem that way from where I'm standing."

"What?" She uninterestedly waved her hands. "You know what? You're very weird, little fish. Just do me a favor and leave me alone."

She turned around and took a few cautious steps back to the beach, on the path of rocks.

"Aldan."

Iara looked at him, raising an eyebrow.

"What?"

"My name is not little fish. It's Aldan."

"That's a weird name. You're not from around here, are you?" He shook his head. "Thought so."

He dove in again and weirdly didn't resurface nearby. So she resumed her walk.

The next few days were a little more complicated at work; the order of new clothes had arrived and the team had to reorganize the entire store. Therefore, Iara ended up not going to the beach for a while, but when she finally went, there he was, the weird boy, far away from everyone else, following her with his eyes. And that was when she decided she had had enough. The boy couldn't get a clue!

In the late afternoon of the following Sunday, she went to the beach, but this time she had her cousin with her for moral support. Both of them got to the beach and Iara soon saw the weird boy, showing Isabella his location without pointing at it. It was easy; he was the one who was further away from everybody else, so far away that only surfers would dare to go there.

The girls calmly walked down the beach, moving towards the rocks on which Iara had climbed the past week.

"Are you getting in the water? I don't think that's a good idea, he is probably a good swimmer since he never leaves the water." Isabella glanced up to where the lonely boy was swimming.

"I thought about the same thing, that's why I'm not going in there."

"Give me your phone, what if he pulls you in or something? If anything happens, I'll scream for help and call the police."

Iara nodded and handed her cousin her phone.

"I don't think it will be necessary, but maybe I'll have to threaten to involve the authorities."

"I hope you don't have to, but good luck."

Iara took a deep breath, preparing herself, then stepped on the wet, rough surface of the rocks. She made her way to the furthest place the path allowed her to go, the closest place to the open sea; and he soon approached her, knowing she wanted to talk to him like she had done before.

"Didn't I tell you not to stare at me like that? What do you want?"

Aldan shrugged.

"I told you my name, but you haven't told me yours."

Her jaw dropped and, when she finally found her voice, she practically yelled:

"You think I'm gonna give my name out to a creep who keeps chasing me?"

"I can't chase you."

Iara let out a groan and held out her arms towards him.

"That's what you're doing!"

"What do you mean? I'm far away, you're the one who came after me."

"You think I can't see you? You're observing me all the time." She crossed her arms. "Just leave me alone or I'll have to call the cops."

He didn't get apprehensive as she expected him to, only confused. Then he changed the subject.

"You were right. I saw other people on the beach picking up trash, but not many of them."

"There are people who do that for a living, you know?"

"You didn't come every day."

"Of course not, that's not my job. I do it because I want to."

"Why?"

"What do you mean?"

"Why did you decide to start doing it?"

Iara opened her mouth and closed right after. She debated whether she should keep the conversation going with the insane guy who wouldn't stop staring at her. But, if she was being honest, he had never done anything that crossed the line, he didn't even go after her, he never left the water. Actually, she wasn't even sure she could put the police on it, but she hoped it would scare him off.

"Well...I always liked to walk around the beach, but it was constantly dirty; I didn't like it, and I realized that it wouldn't change anything if I waited around for other people to do it. If I wanted to see any change, I would have to do it myself." She shrugged, lifting her hands like she was asking him to stop. "Look, I'm done, I'm leaving."

As she turned around to head back to the beach, she slipped and fell into the ocean.

The marine current was stronger than she had imagined, leaving her dazed because of the surprise.

Normally, she likes hanging out in the ocean, but, at the time, all she was thinking about was finding the surface, so she opened her eyes, ignoring the nuisance it caused. Bubbles covered her eyes for a few moments, but they soon scattered, allowing her to see ahead.

Iara couldn't believe what she was seeing: the boy had also dived and was looking at her, but the problem lies beneath his waist. It wasn't a swimsuit and a pair of legs, as it would have been expected; he had a tail like a fish—which, by the way, moved. It couldn't be fake if it moved. The shock was so big she involuntarily gasped, swallowing some water in the process, causing her lungs to burn.

Aldan held his hands out and took her by the arms to take her to the surface. She coughed a few times and took a deep breath, forcing herself to speak in a broken voice—that would have been louder if her throat wasn't aching.

"You're a mermaid?!" She tried to get away, swimming the other way.

"A merman."

That correction came so naturally and seriously to

him that he couldn't be joking around.

Iara was so incredulous that she couldn't even form sentences. So she swam back to the rocks and quickly climbed up them. At the beach, Isabella worriedly watched the scene. To calm her down, Iara gave her a thumbs up signaling she was okay, despite not being so sure of it herself, shivering and not because of the cold.

Aldan disappeared beneath the water once again and came to the surface holding Iara's flip-flops. She was still shaken by all this, so she just moved away from him, which made him leave the flip-flops on the rocks by her side and dive back into the ocean. Looking more carefully, she saw his tail at the moment he submerged, before vanishing down below.

Iara grabbed her flip-flops and got up with her wobbly legs, getting out of there as soon as she could.

Iara didn't tell her cousin or anyone else what she had seen. They would have thought she was insane. Instead, she just said she had fallen, and he had helped her, and maybe he had understood her message to keep his distance.

She didn't go back to that place for a few days, still trying to understand what had happened. What she had seen could have only been a prank, and that's what she was telling herself.

Iara went back to the beach days later and didn't see Aldan at all. And that was repeated throughout the week, when she returned to her walks on the sand in the late afternoon. Until one day, weeks later, when she saw in the ocean, far away from everyone and even further away than any surfer. She couldn't see his face from where she was standing, but she just knew it was him. After all, who else would have been in a place like that?

The fear she felt before had vanished during the weeks that passed by and had been substituted by an insatiable curiosity. She threw out the plastic bag with the trash she had picked up in it and headed down to the rocks once again. When Iara arrived at the furthest point the rock allowed, Aldan cautiously approached her.

"You don't seem as scared now," he commented.

"I don't think I'm still scared, I don't know. Was it a dream?"

"No. You're the first human who I've ever talked to. Are you land people always this weird?"

"Some are weirder, some are less." Her head was still spinning around just from thinking about his origins. She put her flip-flops aside, on a higher part of the rocks so they wouldn't be taken by a stronger wave, and sat down with her feet in the water. The curiosity was eroding her as she focused on his body hidden by the sea. "Can I see your tail?"

Despite finding the request odd, he lifted the tip over the water. Iara held out her hand, touching the wet scales. It was almost as if there was a giant fish beneath her fingers, and it was dark green like Aldan's eyes.

"Is it really real?" She still couldn't believe it.

"Why wouldn't it be?"

"Because...because you don't exist! Or weren't supposed to exist."

"I do exist, yes, and there are many others. You don't see us because we have decided to stay away from you and we live in the depths of the sea. Don't you remember where you guys came from?"

"What do you mean?"

"Humans came from the sea. Everything came from the sea. Way before the land divided itself and created continents, the landmass was only one, surrounded by only one ocean, as well as the people who lived in it. However, disagreements divided opinions and generated fights between the people. Half of them wanted to stay in the depths and the other half sought the air from the surface. This group lost their scales and got a pair of legs. That's you."

She shook her head.

"No, that doesn't make any sense. And why are you here after all?"

"I was angry and tired of seeing what humans do to our home, littering and making our animals sick. I wanted to understand the reason behind it all. Why did humans hate us so much? But, from what I've seen in many different places, is that actually, they don't try to spoil everything, at least not most of them. They simply don't care, as you told me on the first day I got here on this beach. And you were one of the few who did something about it."

"Is that why you wouldn't stop observing me? Because what I was doing was rare?"

"Because you were unique and interesting." She smiled at the compliments. "And even fought me because of the reason that brought me to the surface. That was very unexpected to me." He finished with a small laugh.

"That was because you threw a bottle at me! I thought you were messing with me. I could've sworn you were a spoiled kid, who kept trashing the beach like everyone else." Her voice was gone, when it returned, she changed the subject. "I know it doesn't seem like it, but there are a lot of people out there who care about the environment," she paused, but he cut her off before she could continue.

"There are also a lot of people who don't." His eyes traced her up and down, then looked away. "I've lost count of how many pieces of plastic I've taken off of animals. I even thought of asking people why they did it, because I wanted to understand, but I wasn't brave enough to do it." He shrugged.

"And you shouldn't be. If you had been seen by the wrong people, they could've captured you and done experiments on you to make money. It would've been a total chaos.

"That's horrible, you are all so weird." Aldan scowled, drifting back slightly. "It wasn't for nothing that our Elders forbade us to come to the surface."

"Which you are completely ignoring right now, huh?"

He smiled as a reply.

"What can I say? I think I'm at the age of rebelling."

"You were just curious, that's the truth. If it was a matter of age, a lot of people would've already seen a lot of mermaids and mermen around."

"I think it's more interesting for most of them to stay in the depths of the sea."

"I have to agree. I actually love to stay in the water, it's so nice and relaxing." She looked up. The sky was already getting dark, the sun had already been hidden for a while. "I have to go now. I still have a lot to do."

"Okay. I'll see you tomorrow?"

Iara smiled and nodded before she stood up and took her flip-flops. Waving goodbye, she headed towards the beach.

The work at the store was quite heavy the next day because of the sales season, but the thought of meeting Aldan left her feeling excited enough to drop by the beach before going back home.

She put on her flip-flops and her bag on a rock on the

way and sat on the shore; her brown eyes were sparkling with anticipation to see him again.

Aldan wasn't observing her like before; he couldn't even be seen. However, he soon emerged and swam in her direction.

"You weren't around, how did you find out I was already here?"

"I thought you didn't like it when I watched you from afar, so I was swimming around, but I kept an eye out to see if you had already arrived."

"I see, thank you. By the way, I was thinking about this yesterday. How old are you to be 'at the age of rebellion?'"

"Fifty-seven."

Iara laughed.

"You're kidding, right? You don't even look a day past twenty!"

Aldan shrugged with a smolder. "What can I say? Rumor has it that those who chose the air live less than us."

"Unbelievable!"

"What about you?"

"I'm twenty-three...but, tell me, what is it like living down there? What do like to do for fun?"

"Basically, swimming and exploring new places. The ocean is huge and not even us, who live down there, know everything about it."

"Least of all us! We know more about space than we do about the ocean. It seems really fun." She laughed, looking him up and down. "And you're out there, living MY childhood dream just by existing!"

"What do you mean?"

"When I was a kid, I wanted to be a mermaid. And a fairy."

"A fairy?"

"They're like humans, but they have wings. They're also really tiny, but they don't exist."

"Mermaids exist."

"Yeah." She moved her feet underwater, pulling them out now and then before submerging them again. "Who knows, maybe they do exist, right? But all we know is that they're myths. Anyway, I wanted to be a lot of things. And, of course, I had the professions phase. I wanted to be a vet."

"And why aren't you? That's something you could become, right?"

"Yeah, but I would have to get accepted into university, which didn't happen. I still study by myself, but I can't afford to pay my tuition, and there are no community colleges around here." She shrugged. "I was able to get a job and things started changing. At least I moved out to live with my cousin."

Curious about her, he rested his arms on the rocks by his side. Aldan couldn't and didn't want to hide the smile her mere presence caused.

"Why did you want to move out of your parents' house?"

"I didn't get along very well with my dad and my mom died when I was born. It was chaos."

He nodded, but decided to change the subject, since the conversation was taking a bitter turn. "What about you? What do you do for fun?"

"Not a lot, actually. I work a lot and I don't have as much free time as I would like, but I love coming down here when I'm able to. And I like spending time with my cousin, Isabella, she is my best friend. We like playing board games and cards when we have time to meet other friends. Going to the movies is also nice, but it's been so expensive lately that it's hard for me to go."

"I don't know what any of that is."

"Maybe I'll explain them to you someday. But now I have to go."

"Wait, I have something for you." He dove in before she could say anything, so Iara waited a few minutes until he came back with a spiral seashell that was almost 20 centimeters long. "For you to remember me by when there's nothing but the air surrounding you."

"It's beautiful! Thank you!" Her jaw dropped as she held that perfect seashell. She held it against her ear, which got a confused look from him. "You can hear the ocean in here."

"For real?"

Iara held out the object against his ear and Aldan stopped to hear.

"I think you haven't realized it yet for being in there, but the echo the shell makes is similar to the sound of the waves crashing against the shore."

"It really does."

"Well then, I'll see you tomorrow." Biting her lower lip to help contain a smile, she stood up carefully holding her gift, following the way back home.

Isabella, curious, wanted to know the reason behind her cousin's sudden happiness, accompanied by a seashell that was hard to find. Iara had to find a way to explain it without mentioning her new friend's tail.

After that, she met Aldan almost every single day at the same place by the rocks.

The days were going by and turning into weeks, which turned into months, both of them feeling even closer to each other as time went by. Sometimes she would show him part of her world on the tiny phone screen, and other times he would bring his friends for her to meet. That's how she got to make her dream of swimming with dolphins come true. Sometimes, when she wouldn't bring her bag or phone, she would wear a swimsuit so she could swim with the merman, usually on the weekends.

On a Sunday, she arrived a little earlier than usual to spend more time with him. This time, she had come with a bikini under her clothes; she took them off and left them on the rocks. She hadn't even brought her cellphone. Walking to the edge of the rocky path, Iara didn't even notice Aldan's eyes tracing her up and down with his eyes.

She put her feet inside the water, then went further, first the knees, later the legs until she went all the way down. Despite the sun shining on them and the nice weather, she shivered, getting used to the water's temperature.

He shifted closer to the open sea and extended his hand to her. She raised hers and accepted the gesture; in return, he drew her to him. Iara forgot the coldness once her body was pressed against his smooth skin. She bit her lower lip.

Aldan swam calmly, and she relaxed in his embrace. It was so comfortable. Iara only realized they had gone so far away when the sun was going down and the lights on the tiny shore were on. Her jaw dropped.

"How am I gonna be able to swim back? The current is pulling us to the opposite side, isn't it?"

"Yeah, how did you notice?"

"That was the direction we naturally went without even realizing it."

"I did. I can naturally feel the current. The water has a life of its own and it goes wherever it wants to go. The people of the sea had to learn how to feel it. To go back, we just have to swim diagonally. But don't worry, I'm not gonna let anything bad happen to you." So, Aldan started swimming, taking her with him.

Iara also helped and, moving her hands in the water, she imagined how it must be for him to feel it moving; *was it like feeling the direction in which the wind blows?* she asked herself.

Aldan calmly swam, and even so, he was fast and precise. It couldn't have been different with so many years of practice.

"Iara, I've seen humans with their faces touching each other's a few times. Why do you do that?"

She held a small laugh.

"I think you're talking about a kiss. It's one of the ways we have to show affection to the people we're more emotionally involved with. You guys don't do it?"

"Not like that."

"How do you do it, then?"

"By 'invading' each other's personal space and interlocking our tails. Kind of like this." He brought his tail closer to her legs, and that startled her a little.

"That feels different."

"Is this kiss thing any good?"

"Maybe I can show you." Iara held his face softly and leaned in, so her lips could touch his.

Aldan was taken by surprise at first but soon closed his eyes, enjoying the moment and being delighted by the weird human form of affection. With a hand sliding to her waist, he pulled her even closer to him; the other hand went to her long straight hair, tugging it slightly. His heart was beating so fast he forgot everything else; all that mattered was her sweet tongue against his.

Her skin tingled wherever his hands touched, sending energizing waves all over her. Iara had kissed other men before, but none had made this fuzzy warmth radiate throughout her body the way Aldan did.

"This is...interesting." He said as they parted from the kiss, not wanting to let her go anymore.

She smiled as a reply, enjoying it as much as he did to the point of being breathless. They were both close enough to the rocks that she was able to head back to the beach. The summer nights weren't as cold, so she wasn't bothered by the wind as she got out of the water. She said goodbye once again and went home.

It shouldn't have been so hard for Iara to take each step, and she wasn't supposed to be so surprised by what happened, but that day's events made her reflect upon them the whole night, looking at a part of the ocean she could see through her window. What was she doing with Aldan? Did she really want a relationship? How could this work if she couldn't even introduce him to her friends; except for maybe a few trustworthy people if Aldan accepted it? What if she found a good job in a non-coastal city?

Iara would never be able to have a normal life with him; she'd have to work hard to support herself, only to be able to see him at the beach at the end of the day, hiding him from everyone she knew. Not to mention the risk of him being seen by curious people and attracting negative attention.

By the time she made a hard decision, the sky was already light blue. With a heavy sigh, she changed her clothes and went to work.

When she met Aldan in the late afternoon, her heart was still distressed and he noticed it as soon as he saw her.

"What's wrong?"

"I..." She gulped, impatiently moving her feet underwater. "I think it's best for us not to see each other again. This isn't gonna work. It's impossible. We're just gonna get hurt."

"Don't say that. The time we spend together is amazing."

"That's the reason why. A bird can love a fish, but where would they live?" She summarized the problem with an analogy taken from an old movie.

He understood what she meant by that and held her hand, looking deep into her eyes.

"Then let's give the bird some scales, or give the fish wings."

She tilted her head.

"What do you mean by that?"

"It's rare, but it's possible for one to follow the other. I could go to the land, or you could come to the sea. I can give up my scales, or I can give you your own."

"For real?" She murmured and he nodded.

"This has happened before, with a friend of my grandma's. However, she wasn't innocent to think that would happen without giving something in return."

"What is the price?"

He gulped. His voice sounded calm and sober.

"First of all, there is no going back. If you want to come to the sea, the transformation is gonna hurt, but, if you have a good heart, you will be successful. And I know you do. Besides, all you need is a little blood from someone who was born in the ocean, and half of their life."

Her jaw dropped.

"You would give me half of your life?"

He interlocked his fingers with hers. Iara's skin still tingled under his touch.

"I would give you everything."

"I can't allow you to give up half of your life, even if you live a lot longer than humans do. That wouldn't be fair."

"I wouldn't be giving it up, I would be giving it to someone who matters to me more than anything. Seems fair to me."

Her heart started beating overwhelmingly fast, in a mixture of shock and flattery.

"What if you come to the land?"

"You would have to give me a little of your blood, a cut on your hand is enough. And the same thing happens with the transformation, and my lifespan would be like the one of a human."

"What would you like to do?"

"Whatever you want. If you want to come to the sea, I'll help you get used to the depths, just like I'm sure you will be by my side if I go to the land."

"What about the people from the sea? Would they accept me easily? Your parents too?"

"When the transformation is done, they have to accept it. And as for my family, they will have to accept it too. The people from the sea only truly love once." He gently squeezed her hand. "And my heart chose you."

Iara was moved by Aldan's direct sincerity and leaned in for one more kiss.

"I love you too."

Iara looked at her feet underwater and then to the city behind her, pondering. Did she have that much to lose?

"I think the only person I'm really gonna miss is my cousin. She has always been by my side when I needed it, she's my best friend. And I didn't even tell her about your origins."

"She will have to know." Understanding where the conversation was going, he added. "And it doesn't mean you'll never get to see her again, but it would be pretty hard to do it."

"I know." A tear rolled down her face and Aldan held out his hand to wipe it off, getting her face even wetter. Iara didn't mind. When she continued, she had already decided what to do. "I want to come to the sea. And how long will we be able to live for?"

"We can't be sure, but I'm assuming for about a hundred years from now on. And then we will become sea foam."

"Is that what happens to the people from the sea?"

He nodded.

"And I know it's not as long as mine would have been, but it will be full and complete because I like myself better when I'm with you."

"Me too."

"That being said, I will come back in three days to take you to the depths of the sea."

With a last kiss goodbye, she went back home, and he dove back in.

Iara didn't have the heart to tell Isabella, knowing very well that her cousin would think she had gone insane, to say the least. Not because she was running away with a boy—that wouldn't even be the worst part—but where he was taking her.

Thus, she quit her job and spent her whole free time with her cousin and her friends. Iara explained everything through a note she would leave on her bed, revealing all the secrets and leaving her few belongings to Isabella. She didn't need them where she was going.

She said goodbye to Isabella, knowing she would find

her note in the right moment, and headed one last time to the rocks on the beach. As expected, Aldan was waiting for her.

"Are you ready?" He asked her one last time.

"Yes."

He held out his hand to her.

"Then come with me."

Iara took off the clothes she wouldn't need anymore, leaving them on the rocks, and got in the water. If the tide didn't take them away or if they weren't stolen, Isabella would find them and she would know everything was true.

"What now?"

"You drink this and dive in." He gave her a little bottle with a purple liquid inside. "You will feel like you're drowning for a moment, but everything is gonna be okay and I'll be right by your side."

Iara nodded and followed his instructions. The transformation, as he said, was painful and she couldn't breathe for a while, which seemed way too long. And then it passed. It was over and she had never felt that comfortable underwater. It was like she had been waiting for this her entire life without knowing.

Euphoric, she kissed Aldan once again and he—holding her hand—guided her to the bottom of the sea.

Made in the USA
Columbia, SC
08 February 2021